The Somebodies

ALSO BY N. E. BODE

THE ANYBODIES
THE NOBODIES

The Somebodies

by N. E. Bode

Illustrated by PETER FERGUSON

HARPERCOLLINSPUBLISHERS

Library of Congress Cataloging-in-Publication Data

Bode, N. E.

The Somebodies / N. E. Bode ; illustrations by Peter Ferguson.— 1st
ed.

    p.   cm.

Summary: Continuing her magical adventures, Fern travels with
Howard to an underground city to save the Anybodies from the
horrible Blue Queen, who sucks the souls out of books.

ISBN-10: 0-06-079111-X (trade bdg.)

ISBN-13: 978-0-06-079111-7 (trade bdg.)

ISBN-10: 0-06-079112-8 (lib. bdg.)

ISBN-13: 978-0-06-079112-4 (lib. bdg.)

[1. Magic—Fiction. 2. Books and reading—Fiction. 3. Queens—
Fiction.] I. Ferguson, Peter, 1968– ill. II. Title.

PZ7.B63362So 2006   2006000356

[Fic]—dc22   CIP

                                        AC

1 2 3 4 5 6 7 8 9 10

First Edition

THIS BOOK IS DEDICATED
to your soul—a stunning soul that is
not in the least bit ordinary

PART 4
The Brain

PART 5
The Secret Society of Somebodies

A LETTER FROM N. E. BODE

Oh, smart and witty reader, so brave and true-hearted—
I think of you more often than you think of me.
I do.

I wonder if you've had a good day. Have you found a dollar in an empty bus seat, gotten six chicken nuggets in your five-pack, been told you arm-wrestle so well you could become famous for it? Or are you having a bad day—suffered a noogie, swallowed gum, eaten a bad taco?

I've known bad days. You see, my insanely jealous creative writing professor, whose name I will not disclose, has recently won a Guggenpulitzheimer, the famous, coveted literary prize. Maybe you've heard him speak on the radio—long, windy speeches on his own rare talent and the benefits of having been born with a full set of pearly baby teeth, et cetera. I thought this bit of fame might lighten him up a little. But, alas, no. By the time I'd finished writing *The Anybodies* and was working on *The Nobodies*—both of which describe the all-true adventures of Fern and Howard—I was *still* dodging his vicious bunny attacks and his purposefully misguided wrecking balls. And I had resorted to living a haunted life in various disguises: rodeo clown, brain surgeon, fishmonger—you get the idea. My rare joy was when I called my editor on a pay phone and asked that she read me my fan mail. (Hello, Jack Reilly from Elsmere! Hello, Ursula the Brave and Leah of the breathless sentences! Hello, bitter nitpicker who fussed at me for ending my sentences with prepositions—thanks for noticing!) These joys were fleeting.

Shortly after I finished writing the stories of Fern and Howard, who are as smart and witty and brave and true-hearted as you, I became a shaking mess. I'd been hiding out and I'd been very sickly. I had no idea why I'd been so weak and exhausted and pale—a mere ghost of my true self. I thought perhaps the constant fear of my creative writing professor was getting to me. But, as Fern would later explain, I was caught up in something else, something much bigger and more sinister, something that had to do with Anybodies, as well as the Somebodies and the dastardly Blue Queen!

But I'm getting ahead of myself here. I only learned all this after Fern got word to me through a company called Super Jack's Singing Carrier Pigeon Telegram Message Service. The pigeon had a note attached to his little leg and tweeted, singishly, while I read.

In the note Fern explained that she and Howard had gone through a new adventure, and my sickness was a part of it all. Of course, I really wanted to write all about this adventure too, but I didn't know how I'd be able to, what with my insanely jealous creative writing professor trying to off me at every sharp turn. I needed a safe haven. Happily, Fern and Howard knew the best hiding place in the world. I cannot tell you where—not yet. No, no, no. You've got to be patient for that.

But now, for those who don't know who Fern and Howard are, or what an Anybody is, you don't really have to run back to the first two books, *The Anybodies* and *The Nobodies*. (You can if you want to. Of course I'm not going to stop you!) Here is a short glossary of terms:

1. AN ANYBODY—a person who by nature or training (concentration and sometimes hypnosis) can transform objects into reality (for example, Fern once reached into a painting of a fishpond and petted the fish) and who can transform themselves and others (a nun into a lamppost, a bad guy into a bull). Anybodies are shape changers in a way, as you'll see, who are so in tune with the world's constant state of change—the world is always changing, you know, and nothing stays the same—that Anybodies can change right along with it.

2. FERN—A girl who found out, not too long ago, that she was swapped at birth, and she isn't the daughter of a pair of tragically dull accountants, the Drudgers, as she'd always thought. She's actually an Anybody, and a royal Anybody, in fact. At the end of Fern's exhausting but heroic summer camp adventure, her precious book, *The Art of Being Anybody*, had given Fern the crown and scepter, and the person who owns the crown and scepter is the royal ruler.

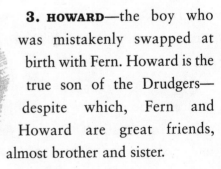

3. HOWARD—the boy who was mistakenly swapped at birth with Fern. Howard is the true son of the Drudgers—despite which, Fern and Howard are great friends, almost brother and sister.

4. THE BONE—Fern's father. He was a washed-up Anybody who never was naturally gifted, and he now lives with Fern and Fern's grandmother in her grandmother's boardinghouse.

5. ELIZA—Fern's mother. She was a great Anybody. She died while giving birth to Fern, but Fern still feels her mother's presence strongly and often smells the scent of lilacs—Eliza's favorite flower—pouring out of her mother's old diary.

6. THE GREAT REALDO—the greatest of all Anybodies, the Great Realdo is a force for good, and the current Great Realdo is, in fact, Fern's grandmother, Dorathea Gretel. Have some fun and shove around the letters in "the Great Realdo" and you might come up with "Dorathea Gretel."

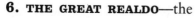

5

7. *THE ART OF BEING ANYBODY* BY OGLETHORP HENCEFORTHTOWITH—a one-of-a-kind book that holds all the secrets of being an Anybody and that can only be read by the person who the book belongs to. The book belongs to Fern, but she has had to keep it out of the hands of two bad guys back-to-back: the Miser and <u>BORT</u>.

8. FERN'S GRANDMOTHER'S BOARDINGHOUSE—a house that exists in a world of books. It's even constructed with books as the main building supply! The house is populated with creatures that have been shaken from books—Borrowers in the walls, hobbits in the yard, Indians in the cupboards. It's situated where the sidewalk ends, beside a peach tree with the most enormous, one might say, *giant* peach.

9. THE SOMEBODIES—well, I can't tell you who the Somebodies are, can I? That would ruin this book!

Okay, okay, enough dillydallying and lollygagging, not to mention dillylolling and dallygagging. Turn the page!

From my hidden perch,

NE Bode

THE CITY BENEATH THE CITY

THE NIGHT BEFORE THE ANNUAL ANYBODIES Convention, Fern sat on the book-lined stairs of her grandmother's boardinghouse. She was eavesdropping on the heated argument in the kitchen. It was after dinner and stew smells hung in the air—all beefy and porky and, well, stewy. Fern couldn't make out every word of the argument. The boardinghouse was like a big ear stuffed with cotton—so crammed with books that sounds were muffled. (In fact, the staircase was like an upward tunnel through a mound of books that someone had dug their way out of.) Making the eavesdropping harder, the hobbits who lived in homes of grassy mounds out in the yard were singing what sounded like sea shanties, and the Indian, who usually

9

lived in the cupboard, was playing a drum of some sort. Fern could only hear the argument when Dorathea and the Bone raised their voices.

"Fern needs to be among *[muffle, muffle]* Anybodies," the Bone said. "We must face the fact that she's royal now!" the Bone shouted.

This was true. Fern balled up her fist and shook it. "I'm royal now," she whispered urgently. "You tell her!"

Dorathea didn't like the fact that Fern was royal. *It's too soon,* her grandmother had told her. *You aren't ready.* But the Bone was proud and loved the idea of being royal-by-association. He'd grown up quite poor and lonesome, you see—the son of a fat lady in a circus. "What will it hurt her to miss a few days of long division?" the Bone said.

"Yes, yes!" Fern said. "What good is long division?"

Fern could hear dishes rattling in the sink. "She needs to know *[clank, clank]* . . . live in the real world," Dorathea was saying. "Royalty *[muffle, muffle]* . . . it won't do her any good at this point. It will just *[loud chorus of sea shanty and drumming]* . . . and spoil her."

But what if Fern wanted to be spoiled? She kind of did, and who could blame her, really? I want to be spoiled— velvet pillows, and miniature claw-footed bathtubs just for my feet, and chocolates in the shapes of squirrels or porcupines, life-sized, or whatever it is that the rich have nowadays. "Don't underestimate the importance of long division, and a real childhood," Dorathea said.

The argument was about whether or not Dorathea should take Fern to the Annual Anybodies Convention, which was always held at Willy Fattler's Underground Hotel, located near New York City.

Let me be more accurate: Willy Fattler's Underground Hotel isn't *near* New York City as much as it is *under* New York City, which is how it got the "Underground" part of its name.

Everyone knows that New York has a lot going on underground. Its subway cars with their shiny poles are filled with all kinds of people and their hats, shopping bags, umbrellas, schnauzers, and portable massage tables, all jiggering down dark. tunnels into their unknowable futures. In fact, as this story starts, I was one of those New Yorkers—in disguise so that I could dodge my insanely jealous creative writing professor's murderous plots, of course! Imagine me holding on to the shiny subway pole, dressed as a confused bishop in a tall white pointed hat, or an elderly woman feeding Yum-Yums to her pet Chihuahua, its bony head poking out of her black pocketbook, or a sushi chef (which is very hard to say three times fast). I had no idea that, just below, there was a city beneath the city, an Anybody city, a shorter, more bulbously rotund version of New York City. This city beneath the city was warped, because it had to grow around steam pipes, aqueducts, and abandoned chutes of all sorts, the buildings twisting the way roots grow around water pipes. Its sky was dirt-packed and veined with the undersides of subway tunnels.

Fern had read all about the city beneath the city in *The Art of Being Anybody*—Chapter 16, "Anybody Locales," which featured a large, leathery foldout map. It wasn't just a crisscross of street names—6th and Apple, 32nd and Small Change—like a normal map. No, no. It included the names of the shops and buildings: Hoist's Deli, Melvin's Laundromat and Dry Cleaner's, Hyun's Dollar Fiesta. There were a few squat churches and synagogues, a portly mosque, a row of narrow courthouses, and a castle with a gate and a short pointy spire, which poked right into the dirty underside of Manhattan like a tack on a rumpy teacher's chair.

Fern was desperate to go to the city beneath the city, mainly because it was chock-full of Anybodies—a whole city of people like her, with her powers. She wanted to see exactly what such a place would be like, especially now that she spent most of her time clamped into a desk, surrounded by kids who didn't know that Anybodies existed, and taught by the brooding, whirling, yammering Mrs. Fluggery (who'd already accused Fern of having a head stuffed with doilies).

Doilies? Yes, doilies. Mrs. Fluggery was odd. She often didn't make any sense at all. She stuffed dirty tissues up her sleeves and had hair in the airy shape of

12

the Washington Monument.

All day long Fern had to forget that she was an Anybody. She hated the rows of desks all shoved together, the kids all poking at one another and being mean, not to mention the gummy underside of everything. The kids were all smiley and do-right in front of the teacher, but then turned on you, ready to pinch or knuckle-punch—especially Lucess Brine (pronounced LOO-sess) or Lulu, as she liked to be called, even though it was a nickname that didn't fit her and no one ever called her that. Lucess was also a new student that year. She was a strange kid. Fern had never met anyone like her before. She was a bully, but apologetic about it. She sat behind Fern and would pinch her in the back and tattle on Fern for the littlest things, like pulling the eraser out of her pencil or putting the wrong date on her paper. Then sometimes Fern would find a note from Lucess in her pocket later, saying something like:

Fern,

I'm sorry I did that. I can't help it. I'm no good. (Do you feel sorry for me now?)

And don't tell anyone I apologized to you or I'll pinch you harder next time! Don't you wish you were a somebody, like me, not a big-eyed freaky nobody, like yourself? (Did that make you feel bad?)

Lucess

The notes were always pretty much the same. Sometimes Lucess called Fern a "big-haired freaky nobody," but that was a rare deviation. It seemed like every time Fern turned around, Lucess Brine's perky nose was aimed right at her, and Lucess was bragging about something—her glitter lip gloss, her house with its multiple refrigerators, or her mother's rubber fruit collection. "It's so real that our tax man nearly choked to death on a blue grape!" Most of her bragging had to do with Lucess's mother, who, she claimed, was tall, elegant, beautiful, rich. She seemed to like to bring up her mother, and then turn to Fern, saying, "Awww, sorry, I forgot. You don't have one. Isn't that a sore spot with you?"

And all of Lucess's friends would laugh. Lucess seemed to have tons of friends even though she wasn't particularly nice to them either—at least not in public. Lucess was one of those nasty kids who other kids are attracted to, out of awe or fear.

Lucess made Fern want to brag in other ways. Fern had a lot to brag about. She was a gifted Anybody who'd once turned herself into a grizzly bear! Could Lucess Brine's rich mother with her rubber fruit collection compete with that? But Fern wasn't allowed to say anything like this. She just had to nod and say, "Congratulations on almost choking the tax man."

Fern had to try to be somewhat ordinary again, and Fern wasn't very good at being ordinary. She'd tried it,

14

and it always made her feel clamped down, like a bunny in a shoe box. This was frustrating, because she wanted to be a great Anybody. She was royalty, after all. And great Anybodies tended to be their own people. They didn't fit in. They seemed to get down to what was essential them—their unique core—and build themselves up from there. What if her grandmother had walked around just trying to be ordinary? Would she have become the Great Realdo? What if the hermit, Phoebe, had just tried to fit in? Would she ever have learned how to travel through a teapot to London, where she and Holmquist were now on their honeymoon? Take the great Willy Fattler, genius of Willy Fattler's Underground Hotel. What if he'd tried to be average? Would he ever have designed the wildest ever-changing Anybody hotel of all time? The answers to these questions were: no, no, and no.

Howard, on the other hand, had been the one to love being ordinary. He was wonderful at it. After the harrowing adventures of camp, he'd requested to spend the rest of the summer with the Drudgers, his biological parents, so that he could get a bellyful of ordinary. He promised not to do any Anybody trickery (he'd once accidentally turned them into monkeys while showing off for a friend), and this time he'd stayed true to his word. He just enjoyed his math books and the bland food and the beige walls and the beige carpeting, and his parents, Mr. and Mrs. Drudger. He adored listening to them discuss all their favorite things: sod, coupons, desk organizers, the steam function on their new iron, and tax code. They were both accountants working for Beige & Beige. Howard wanted to be an accountant too.

By summer's end the Drudgers and Dorathea and the Bone had decided that it was important that Howard and Fern continue to have a good brotherly, sisterly relationship. They weren't brother and sister, but each was an only child, and so it was important, they all agreed, for the two kids to stick together. To keep up the good relationship they'd developed while at camp together, it was best to have them in the same school. Howard sat two rows to Fern's left, in fact, in Mrs. Fluggery's classroom.

But this didn't help much. Just by sitting there in his dullish Howard way—something Fern had grown oddly fond of—Howard reminded Fern of all of the adventures they'd had together: the rhino that had stampeded out of a book, the attack of the vicious mole, the boat ride down the Avenue of the Americas while it was flooded.

And remembering all these adventures only made Fern want to have another adventure. She wanted to go to the Annual Anybodies Convention in the city beneath the city. She needed to go.

But the conversation in the kitchen had grown quieter,

turned to whispering. It had taken on an urgent, serious tone. And even though the hobbits had stopped singing, Fern couldn't hear anything but hissed bits of speech. She climbed down the stairs and, with her back to the book-covered walls, she slipped toward the kitchen.

"Now isn't the time," Dorathea was saying. "Dark things are happening. Anybodies are in danger. Fern will be a target. Dead books *[muffle, hiss, clank]*."

"Dead books?" the Bone asked.

"Haven't you heard?" Dorathea asked.

Silence.

"As you well know, books have souls. Writers stitch a bit of their souls into them when they write them. *[Muffle]*. Except those books that don't *[muffle, clank]*. . . . The ones made to look like all the others. Ghostwritten celebrity books, those fluffy, mushy romances by . . . *[water running]*, and those sappy books that always want to teach kids a lesson!" Dorathea's tone had turned sour, and who could blame her? No one wants to be taught a lesson, as if reading were only an opportunity to be scolded.

"What you're saying though is that someone's taken the bits of souls out of the books with souls and now they're dead?"

"Dead as doornails. No life in them at all. It's completely new. Totally baffling the authorities . . . *[muffle]* . . ."

Fern had never heard of dead books. She supposed that she did know, in her own intuitive way, that some books were soulless to begin with, those awful books out there that made people like reading a little less. (And I, too, know dull, boring, windy books—do I even have to mention the beastly work of my creative writing professor and his soulless pontificating?) But Fern had never known that books could die. It was an awful thought.

"Where were the books?" the Bone asked.

"In an abandoned apartment building near Fattler's Underground Hotel."

"Who could be responsible?"

"Well, the main suspect has to be the Blue Queen. I don't know of any other Anybody who would do such a horrible thing. She's proven herself capable of murder already, and because she was stripped of all her Anybody powers years ago, after [muffle], she has a motive to want to steal souls from books. She'd have to be working with someone, though, someone who is helping her get started."

"Why, though?"

"Could be that she's storing up—hoarding the power of all those souls—so that she can use all the might at once. Someone's got to stop her, but . . ." There was a lull, like Dorathea didn't want to go on with her thought, but she did. "The Blue Queen is a good bit younger than I am. I don't think I can defeat her. I have to face the fact that I'm getting older now. This will be a battle of brute force."

"And Fern is too young," the Bone said.

"Of course she is!"

I am not too young, Fern thought. *I could do it!* But then in the next breath, she thought, *They're right. I can't. I'm too young.* Fern was of that age, you know the one: half the time you're old enough to do so much more than you're allowed, and then the other half of the time you're pushed to do things you aren't quite old enough to do yet. A frustrating pinch to be in—a sprawl of time that actually lingers for years, and unfortunately, in some adults for decades. Sometimes Fern found herself feeling both ways at the same time: *I'm old enough, but, no, I'm not.* This was one of these times. Her conflicting emotions, however, were over-whelmed by a sense of sadness. Her grandmother being too old to really take command as she once had as the Great Realdo, and Fern being too young . . . well, it brought up the fact that her mother was missing. Her mother could have defeated the Blue Queen, surely.

Fern slid along the wall and up the staircase as quietly as she could. She walked into her room and shut the door. *Dead books, the Blue Queen*—the words rang in her mind like the awful *gong* of a bell. She opened the bottom drawer of her dresser, dug underneath two stacks of sweaters, and pulled out her crown and scepter. She had to go to this convention in Willie Fattler's Underground Hotel. She could help put an end to dead books. She could help defeat the Blue Queen, whoever the Blue Queen was. Fern wanted to be a hero. It was her responsibility, wasn't it? Her duty.

The crown was too big, but it was beautiful: heavy gold lined with velvet. The scepter was heavy too. She picked up *The Art of Being Anybody*, flipped it to Chapter 16, and opened the foldout map. She traced the streets, letting her finger rest a minute on Willy Fattler's Underground Hotel. She was desperate to see it with her own eyes. She knew from Dorathea that his hotel was always changing in a liquidlike shifting. It was one hotel, and yet at the same time it was all hotels, and no other Anybody had the skill to do such a thing, let alone the large-hearted generosity to open the place to the Anybody world. There was a picture of Fattler, his mouth wide open as if in mid oration, and his waxy moustache, large and upturned, curling at either cheek. He was a genius in a long line of geniuses.

Fern traced the winding roads on the map, and all the shops like Melvin's Laundromat and Dry Cleaner's and Hyun's Dollar Fiesta, the ballpark, the churches and synagogues, the mosque. And then the castle—its filigree gate, its grillwork clock, the grassy mound on the front lawn, and the pointy spire on top gouging the dirt of Manhattan. She pictured them all down there, oblivious to the return of the Blue Queen. She closed the map and flipped to the back of the book to find the Blue Queen's listing in the index. She turned to the entry. Like all of Henceforthtowith's writing, it was hard to read.

Firstly indignifamously known for evilous plots and dastardhatchschemery, the Blue Queen, neretowith, took over—in villainous piratry—the Anybodies, synchronimously with the death of the Great Realdo's heir. The Blue Queen had wed Merton Gretel—youngest brother to Dorathea, the Great Realdo—to gain advantageous grip-hold on the ruling family. Hitheryon, she overtook the castle, squatted, and relegated regally from thither, beknowst in proclaimation as: The Eleven Days and Nights of Blue Reign. It was a recoil into monarchy.

She hostaged twenty-three persona, hoisted off the street, chained and battened. And all did her bidding, with fleet rectitude, or otherwise were killed—one hostage per day—at her singsong say-so. And if Anybodies didn't do as she said with fleet rectitude, she would kill more (more not merrier in this case). In those short days, 243 statues of the Blue Queen were begun (some halfishly remain); her profile-ish face was stamped on stamps, monies, handcarts, wallpaper, linoleum, banana stickers, etc.; a new anthem was heaved over bullcoms and interhorns.

Heavedly and with braverous heart, the Great Realdo brokenly rose from mourning her deceased heir—Eliza in birthing—and with helpful betrayings from Merton, her brother, she overtookturned the Blue Queen's innersquare. Thusly said, and rightly so. Justicely, rightitude was hailed. The Blue Queen was cast outward and devolved of all her powers.

This befuddling information was followed by a list of the dead: Ernst Flank, Marilynn Partridge, Carlita Cole, the Borscht Duo (Irv and Todd), Marge "the Boss" Carter, Olaf Chang, Jive McMurtry, Erma Harris, Albert Jones-Jones . . . Fern's finger ran down the names, and stopped on the last one: Merton Gretel. This was her grandmother's very own younger brother. The Blue Queen married and then killed him? Fern had never heard of him. What was he like? How had he died? Fern knotted her brow and tried to think of some sensible thing this could possibly mean. It seemed that the Blue Queen ruled the Anybodies from the Castle like a monarchy, for eleven days, and that the Great Realdo, Fern's grandmother, defeated her with the help of her younger brother, who was married to the Blue Queen. The Blue Queen was then cast out and stripped of her powers. Was she using the souls of books to bring herself back?

Fern sat there for a moment, staring off into space. She was thinking of her mother. Would she have let Fern go to the convention? Would she have thought that Fern was ready to really help? To be a hero? She wished that she could ask her these questions. She took out a pen from her nightstand and wrote "Merton Gretel" on her hand. She wanted to remember it.

A strange noise interrupted her. A splash. She turned to the painting of three big goldfish in a pond of lily pads. The painting wasn't in motion. It was a painting. Fern wasn't allowed to feed the three goldfish in the painting. Her grandmother didn't want the fish to become spoiled. Sometimes Fern petted the goldfish, however, reaching into the painting's cool water and splashing around. But tonight something was different about the painting. Something Fern couldn't put her finger on until she counted the fish. One, two, three, four.

There was a fourth fish.

It was hovering just below the surface. It was smaller than the others and had a darker orange spot under one of its big eyes, which was now staring at Fern from the side of its head. Another odd thing was that the fish was smiling at her. Fern smiled back. But then the fish smiled wider, showing a mouthful of teeth—a happy, and then very sad, smile. Goldfish aren't supposed to have teeth like that. No, they aren't.

Fern couldn't look any longer. Something was terribly wrong. The fish was watching her like it knew something she didn't, something awful. Had it come here to spy on her? To scare her? To bite her with its teeth?

Fern turned back to the book on her lap. She let the pages flip slowly through her fingers. And that was when she saw a name at the top of a page that caught her eye. It was her own: Fern. How could she be in a book written long before she was born?

But there she was in a picture with the caption, *Fern Drudger née Bone from the line of Gretel*. It was, unfortunately, her school picture from earlier that year. She'd squinted into the lens—an old habit that came back when she was trying to seem normal. Her hair was pinched down with a barrette—another attempt at blending in. A long time ago, before she'd ever seen a picture of her real mother (who had big eyes and kinked hair), she would have thought this was a good picture. But now she hated how fake it seemed.

There was a story alongside the picture. Although Oglethorp Henceforthtowith's writing was almost impossible to understand, it was easier this time because Fern knew the story. It was her own story: the swapping at birth was accompanied by a date and a picture of the hospital; finding her father had a date and a picture of the Drudgers' address; defeating the

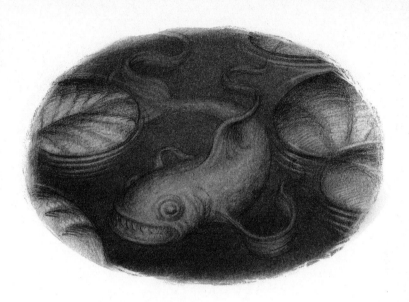

Miser had a date alongside a picture of her grand-mother's house and the abandoned garage, and defeating the evil <u>BORT</u> had a date and a picture of Camp Happy Sunshine Good Times as well as the Fizzy Factory. How could the book have known?

Fern read on and found that the entry didn't stop when she received the crown and scepter. No. She let her index finger slide down the page to the newest entry. Its title made Fern gasp, and jolt up so fast that the crown slipped off her forehead and landed with a soft thud on the bed behind her.

It read *Fern Battles the Blue Queen*.

There was no picture and no date.

At least, not yet.

MRS. FLUGGERY'S RULES AND REGULATIONS

WHEN MRS. FLUGGERY SAID "MRS. FLUGGERY," which she often did—as in, *Mrs. Fluggery doesn't put up with that business!* and *Mrs. Fluggery is displeased!* and *Your bad behavior has forced Mrs. Fluggery to take one of her nitroglycerin tablets!*—a bit of air would collect behind her lips while she was working on the "F" in "Fluggery." This bit of air would inflate her cheeks and even her upper lip above her teeth, and for a brief moment, she would look like a lonesome bullfrog. But then the rest of her name would come tumbling out—"luggery"—and Fern knew that something bad would usually follow. The way Mrs.

Fluggery talked about herself in this detached way gave the impression that the real Mrs. Fluggery was someone else standing just in the hall, behind the door, and she was going to come in and chop everyone to bits with some jujitsu if things didn't change immediately. Mrs. Fluggery only talked about herself as Mrs. Fluggery when she was angry with the class. She was usually angry with the class. And so Fern was nearly always in a wide-eyed state of fear.

I've already mentioned Mrs. Fluggery's monumental hairdo, though Fern preferred the term "hairdon't" as this was such a horrible concoction, and her habit of storing dirty tissues up her sleeve. I've mentioned that she sometimes was forced to take nitroglycerin tablets, because of her heart condition, but I haven't mentioned that the pills—many different bottles of them—clicked in their little containers, and that Mrs. Fluggery sounded like a living maraca every time she took a step. She kept the pills in secret locations all over her person, but mainly in the bulging pockets of her cardigan sweater that stretched taut around her beefy middle.

Her domed stomach was propped up by two spindly legs. I haven't yet mentioned her love of herringbone skirts. Her skirts rode up over her stomach, exposing her bony red knees and, just below them, her knee-high

stockings that sagged around her ankles. And did I
mention that her gauzy hair was
faintly purplish, and not
in a way that seemed
deliberate, like for
example, the hair of
the girl who serves
me cappuccino at
my favorite coffee
shop, Cup O Java,
where I sometimes
go disguised as a
sumo wrestler? No,
no. It was purplish like
skim milk, if skim milk
could be stiffened and placed
on a woman's head. On Mondays
her hair would stand tall, on Tuesdays a little less so, on
Wednesdays a little less so, until Thursdays, when it
was smaller, lumpy, and shaped like a humpbacked
pony. On Fridays her hair collapsed entirely and had to
be propped up by a flimsy scaffolding of bobby pins.
On Mondays it would stand tall again, unless, of
course, she didn't have time to reconstruct it over the
weekend, in which case she'd wear a ski cap.

Mrs. Fluggery had decorated the room with posters

---

explaining her numerous Rules and Regulations. Those on the bulletin board read:

DON'T FIB TO MRS. FLUGGERY. SHE KNOWS WHEN YOU ARE A WORMY LIAR. LEAVE THE LIES AT HOME WITH YOUR PARENTS, WHO TAUGHT SUCH THINGS!

And

DON'T FIGHT. KEEP YOUR DIRTY, STICKY CLAWS TO YOURSELVES! MRS. FLUGGERY DOESN'T WANT TO HAVE TO PULL TWO SUCH BEETLE-EATERS APART!

And

DON'T TALK TO MRS. FLUGGERY ABOUT WHAT YOU WANT TO BE WHEN YOU GROW UP! IT'S RUDE! DO YOU THINK MRS. FLUGGERY WANTED TO BE MRS. FLUGGERY?

Fern tried not to read the posters.

This particular day was a Thursday, but the hump-backed pony hadn't yet shown up in full on Mrs. Fluggery's head. Fern was just starting to be able to make out his hindquarters above Mrs. Fluggery's right ear. She was concentrating on this, ignoring her math problems, letting her eyes blur, when the toothy goldfish swam into her mind. It was quickly followed by the other things she'd heard of last night: dead books, the Blue Queen, Merton Gretel, and *The Art of Being Anybody* knowing that she would battle the Blue Queen. Why hadn't it said that she would *defeat* the Blue Queen? She'd have been more comfortable with that heading. Was it true? Was it about to be historical fact?

This was the moment when Lucess Brine reached under Fern's hooded sweatshirt and pinched Fern in the back. Fern could often squelch a yelp, muffle it, but Lucess was a talented and stealthy pincher. This time she'd twisted the skin just so and Fern had already been in a frightened state of mind. She had to yelp.

The yelp startled Mrs. Fluggery, who turned, with her large, purple-tinged hair and her bulky sweater sleeves, and glared. Mrs. Fluggery clutched her chest. You see, she had a medical condition called angina, and she claimed that sudden disturbances stirred it up.

Lucess Brine said, "Mrs. Fluggery, Fern keeps making noise and it's hard for me to concentrate!"

Lucess had shiny hair that cupped her face. Today was rainy, and she was wearing very expensive galoshes. She'd told everyone that they were the most expensive galoshes her mother could find. Mrs. Fluggery liked Lucess. She said, "When Mrs. F-luggery was a girl, she was much like you, Lucess." And although Lucess would flinch at the comment, she'd quickly change the flinch to a sweet smile as if this were the best thing she'd ever heard.

"Why do you keep bugging me?" Fern whispered. "What did I do to you?" If Fern could tell anyone in the world that she was really royalty, she would pick Lucess Brine, just to see her shocked expression. But, of course, she couldn't, and she knew she should be above wanting to. She knew she should ignore Lucess, not get so upset about her or Mrs. Fluggery. She tried to remain calm.

Lucess whispered quickly, "I'm trying to see what gets to you, what really wears you down."

Fern wanted to ask Lucess why she would want to find out what got to her, why she wanted to wear her down. But Mrs. Fluggery was there. She said, "Mrs. F-"—her face ballooned momentarily—"luggery hopes that you, doily-brain, have just finished the final equation, number one hundred, and that you were so happy, you had to give a little cheer. True or false?"

Fern was supposed to have been doing a worksheet of complex long division, not searching Mrs. Fluggery's hair for a pony. Unfortunately, she was only halfway through number seventeen. She looked at her hands as if she might find the answer there, but she only saw her own handwriting on her palm: Merton Gretel. Could she ask her grandmother about her dead brother? Why hadn't she ever mentioned him before? All these thoughts—all out of place and thrown together—raced through her mind. She stammered a little, closed her hand, and stared down at her nearly vacant paper, dusted with red eraser crumbs.

Mrs. Fluggery said, "Mrs. F-luggery wants the answer to the final question—right now, before Mrs. F-luggery excuses herself to take her heart medication. Do you understand, Little Miss Hampsterhead?"

Howard raised his hand. His hair was freshly trimmed in the style of a middle-aged accountant. He wore a short-sleeved button-down shirt with a fat collar sticking up over a navy sweater vest—in the style of a middle-aged accountant. He often popped breath mints from a tin on his desk, chewing nervously, checking his wristwatch—in the style of a middle-aged accountant. (No need to mention the briefcase.) Howard's eagerly raised hand annoyed Fern a little. Howard always knew the answers, but she also realized that he was trying to come to Fern's rescue. He didn't like to draw attention to himself, especially not Mrs. Fluggery's attention. He wagged his hand over his head in order to cause a distraction. He was a good soul, that Howard.

"Not now, Howard," Mrs. Fluggery said. "Not now!" Mrs. Fluggery walked on her little legs—those sticks that popped out from under the barrel of her belly. "Mrs. F-luggery doesn't like a doily-brain hampsterhead who can't answer a simple question!"

"I'm sorry," Fern said. "I got distracted."

"Distracted!" Mrs. Fluggery screeched. She spun on

her heel and careened around her desk. She threw her arms up and down. "Do you think that Mrs. F-luggery isn't distracted by the fact that her heart is all tightened up? That you children are trying to kill her?" She stopped and leaned on her desk. "Mrs. F-luggery will be back in one-point-five minutes. She is going to the restroom to take her nitroglycerin tablet and to use the facilities, and when she returns, everything must be back in order. Or else . . ."

"Or else what?" Lucess Brine asked.

"Stop it," Fern hissed just loud enough for Lucess to hear.

"Or else Fern and Mrs. F-luggery will have it out in the coatroom!"

A hush fell over the class.

Mrs. Fluggery eyed them all menacingly and then marched out.

Lucess said, "Charlie Barrett has a crooked leg because and he and Mrs. Fluggery had it out in the coatroom. Everyone knows it."

Fern glanced around the room. All the students were nodding except Howard, who shook his head. "You'll be fine, Fern. You've handled worse than her."

"Oh, you have, have you?" Lucess said. "Carson Wilbert won't talk about her cloudy eye. But she had it out with Mrs. Fluggery too."

The other kids whispered fiercely among themselves. Fern heard little echoes of "Charlie Barrett" and "Carson Wilbert"—tales of limps and corrective eyeglasses.

When Mrs. Fluggery walked in, the class stood up and said, in unison, "Good afternoon, Mrs. Fluggery." Although this happened each time Mrs. Fluggery reappeared from one of her nitroglycerin trips to the facilities, Fern thought it was weird. It was as if they'd all decided to pretend that Mrs. Fluggery had just shown up for the first time. Mrs. Fluggery had taught them this. It was one of her Rules and Regulations.

She cast her steely eyes over the class, but said nothing. She picked up a piece of chalk from the silvery ledge and then turned her back to them and began to write.

What the children saw next is almost too awful to say. It was such a horror that I hesitate to go on. It was so ghastly that some of the kids with really frail constitutions (I was once a kid with a frail constitution) went pale and dizzy and almost passed out. You see, Mrs. Fluggery had mistakenly tucked the bottom of her herringbone skirt into her underpants. And so the children, stricken, horrified, saw in a flash her gigantic white underwear with small lavender flowers. They saw the backs of her pale legs, complete with varicose veins, all purple and snakish. She was naked from there on down to her knee-high nylons. It was a ghastly horror, and the students were so shocked that they couldn't breathe or move.

Mrs. Fluggery had written the homework on the board—twenty-one pages of it. She sat down on her vinyl seat. That's when the cold of the vinyl hit her, and she knew the horrible truth. At first she blanched, and then she flushed a deep red. She stood up with her back to the board and rearranged her skirt so that it flopped back into place.

"Mrs. F-luggery," she said, "is deeply disappointed in this class. Not one of you had the courage to tell Mrs. F-luggery of this error. Not one of you! Instead you let Mrs. F-luggery make a fool of herself! You all wanted to be better than Mrs. F-luggery. You wanted to humiliate her. Well, you are a poisoned group of children." She grabbed her chest, pulled out her nitroglycerin tablets and put one under her tongue.

Lucess Brine said ever so quietly—so quietly that Mrs. Fluggery must have imagined it was her very own thought—"Poisoned by. . . ?"

And Mrs. Fluggery's eyes searched the kids as she finished Lucess Brine's sentence. "Fern," Mrs. Fluggery said.

Howard closed his eyes. He couldn't bear to see it. "No, no," he muttered. "Not Fern!"

This caught Mrs. Fluggery's attention. She walked up to Howard, stood before him with her arms crossing her bosom. "And Howard," she said. "Mrs. F-"— Mrs. Fluggery held the captured air of the "F" in her mouth for so long that her face was tight and shining. She emitted a high-pitched squeak. But just when Fern was certain that Mrs. Fluggery was going to blow, the rest of her sentence poured out in a breathless heap: "luggery would like to have it out with you and Fern in the coatroom!"

THE COATROOM

FERN KEPT HER EYES ON MRS. FLUGGERY'S narrow ankles swimming in the bagginess of her knee-high stockings, and followed her—clicking, clicking—to the coatroom. Howard was close behind. Fern thought she heard him sniffle. She hoped he wasn't crying. She didn't want to see him cry. It would make her cry. She was sure of it. She wanted to tell him to be tough. She wanted to say, *Accountants don't cry, Howard,* even though she wasn't sure this was true. She wondered if royalty cry. She'd have to figure that out.

It dawned on Fern, too, that she shouldn't even have to be here. She should have been on her way to the city beneath the city, where she could be useful in important matters like why there are dark winds brewing, and

37

why it's a bad time to be an Anybody, and why there are dead books. She was needed. She was going to battle the Blue Queen, wasn't she? But, no, she was here, marching to the coatroom to get in trouble for something that wasn't really her fault.

The door to the coatroom was brown and covered with one of Mrs. Fluggery's Rules and Regulations posters. This one was devoted to the importance of saying thank you to Mrs. Fluggery. YOU MUST THANK MRS. FLUG-GERY, BECAUSE SHE HAS GIVEN EVERYTHING TO YOU, AND IN FACT, YOU ALL ARE PROBABLY KILLING HER BIT BY BIT!

The coatroom is easy for me to describe. It so happens that I have a lot of experience with coatrooms. My teacher Mrs. Glutten at the Alton School for the Remarkably Giftless put worthless children in the coatroom as a punishment. But because all the students at the Alton School for the Remarkably Giftless were fairly worthless—I, for example, was dim, easily distracted, and occasionally senselessly unruly—all the students were jammed in the coatroom while Mrs. Glutten made extra money as a medical transcriptionist while chain-smoking. (I have used Mrs. Glutten as one of my disguises, minus the pack of Avioli Darks.)

Mrs. Fluggery's coatroom was like most class coatrooms. A small space, its walls covered with coat hooks, most of which had coats dangling from them. It smelled like the gunky heads of schoolchildren. Books and stacked chairs stood in one corner with a janitorial mop and bucket. It was the kind of dirty, moist place where fungi would grow nicely. In fact, Fern was pretty sure that things were growing at this very moment, inside of gym shoes, and greening the edges of bread crusts in forgotten lunch bags. The room had more in common with a terrarium than a normal grown-up coat check of furs and overcoats.

Mrs. Fluggery told Fern and Howard to each get a chair. She pointed to a spot along the wall of hooks. "Put them side by side. Right here."

Howard and Fern did as they were told, and then sat on the chairs.

"No, no, no! Mrs. F-luggery needs to look you in the eye! Stand on the chairs."

Fern and Howard stood, and, both very nervous, they unsteadily climbed up. Fern looked into Mrs. Fluggery's face. She'd never seen it up close before. She noticed the brown spots near the top of her forehead, the pinkness of the loose skin under her chin, the tiny red veins on the sides of her nose. Mrs. Fluggery lifted her gnarled hands with their knotty knuckles, and in one quick motion, she pulled the tags out of the backs of Fern's and Howard's shirts, twisting them over the hooks on the wall behind them. Then she kicked the chairs out from under their feet. They each dropped a few inches, their feet dangling in air as they hung from the coat hooks. "Ha, ha!" Mrs. Fluggery cawed. "Mrs. F-luggery has got you now!"

"This is chaffing me under the arms!" Howard said.

"You can't do this!" Fern shouted. "We have rights, you know!"

"Rights?" Mrs. Fluggery said, and then she turned to a pair of sneakers twisting on the hook near Howard's head. "Do they have rights, Mr. Tennis Shoe? Do they?" She paused. "Speak up! I can't hear you, Mr. Tennis Shoe!" She turned back to the two kids. "Well, well, Mr. Tennis Shoe agrees with Mrs. F-luggery! And Mrs. F-luggery has decided to do this the right way! The old-fashioned way!"

She went to the tallest hook near the stacked chairs, where her own long overcoat was hung. She reached into the sleeve of the coat and pulled out a willow branch.

"What are you going to do?" Fern asked.

"Don't! I'm allergic to pain!" Howard said, and then lost it. He tried to leap off the hook. He tried to run in midair, and then he began banging his fists against the wall and kicking fiercely.

"Howard!" Fern said. "Howard!" She turned back to her teacher. "You, you, you!" Fern said. "Mrs. Fluggery, are a bad, bad teacher! A bad, bad person!"

Mrs. Fluggery turned to Fern. "Mrs. F-luggery is not to be spoken to like that!"

40

Fern looked at Mrs. Fluggery in a way she'd never looked at anyone before—not even the Miser when he was evil, not even the vicious mole BORT when he was attacking. Keep in mind that Fern had transformed books from the imagined to the real—paintings, too. She'd helped her father, with the sheer force of love, to change from the shape of a record player into his real, true form. She herself had turned into a grizzly bear to save a friend. But she'd never done any transformations of any kind from sheer anger.

This was the first.

Mrs. Fluggery jerked her head up, as if trying to see her own stiff monument of hair. Fern looked at her hair too. It was as it had been earlier, the shape of the humpbacked pony not quite there. But then suddenly, out of Mrs. Fluggery's enormous hairdo, an eye peered, and then another.

"Fern," Howard whispered. That was the only sound until a real, albeit miniature, pony whinnied. The pony, with a small hump on its back, was made out of Mrs. Fluggery's hair, and was trapped there, woven into her hairdo, perched on top of Mrs. Fluggery's head. The humpbacked pony shook its mane and tried to rear from its stuck position.

"What?" Mrs. Fluggery screamed. "What is this?"

"I didn't do it!" Fern said, but what she meant was that she hadn't done it on purpose.

The pony bucked again, trying to release itself from Mrs. Fluggery's head. It snorted and pawed Mrs. Fluggery's scalp with its hooves. Mrs. Fluggery was trying to dislodge the pony, but she was tossed around by its weight and roughness. She banged into one wall of coats and then into the stacks of books and chairs.

The janitor's bucket skidded across the room. "My hair!" Mrs. Fluggery said. "Help me!" For the first time in a long time, she wasn't referring to herself as Mrs. Fluggery.

But there was little that Fern and Howard could do. For one thing, they were hooked to the wall, and for another, Fern didn't know how she'd done this in the first place, much less how to undo it.

And then Mrs. Fluggery's face tightened up. She grabbed her heart and fell to the ground in a clatter. The pony was on its side now too, whimpering.

"Oh, no!" Fern cried.

"Do you think she's dead?" Howard asked.

"Put your hands together. Make a cup," Fern said. "Down low so I can put my foot in it and hoist myself off this hook."

Howard did just that, and Fern pushed herself up, and then, once she was loose, she fell to the floor hard. But she landed right near Mrs. Fluggery. She put her hand on the old woman's heart. It was still beating. She put her hand to Mrs. Fluggery's mouth, but she didn't feel any breath. The pony looked weak and sallow. It jerked its head up and down in a sickly fashion, as if it were fading too.

Fern knew what she had to do. She had to put her mouth on Mrs. Fluggery's mouth and breathe the life back into her.

"I have to do it, don't I, Howard?"

"Yep," Howard said, still hooked. "You've got to do it."

She was horrified. She didn't want to put her mouth on Mrs. Fluggery's mouth, which was pruned up, but somewhat open.

Fern bent down. She had to do it. She gave Mrs. Fluggery mouth-to-mouth resuscitation, and Mrs. Fluggery's cheeks blew up with air like a big chalky balloon.

The pony was the first to seem to feel better. His ears pricked up and he tottered around, unhooking himself from Mrs. Fluggery's head. He galloped around the coatroom.

Mrs. Fluggery was next. She woke up with a jolt, her cheeks full-puff. She let out their air and, out of instinct really, said the last part of her name, "luggery," then glanced around the small room, confused as to what had happened.

"You saved her, Fern! You really did!" Howard said, clicking together the heels of his penny loafers from where he hung on the hook. He clapped his hands.

"Saved Mrs. F-luggery?" Mrs. Fluggery said. "For goodness sake, Fern almost killed her!" The old woman stood up, and once again she towered over Fern. She opened the coatroom door and walked between a row of desks. She stumbled a bit, grabbed Horten Everett's head to steady herself, then pulled one of her pill bot-tles from her cardigan sweater's pocket. All the kids were staring up from their desks.

Fern walked over to Howard. She bent down so he could use her back to lift himself off the hook. The two of them stepped out of the coatroom.

"You two are expelled! You'll never step foot in Mrs. F-luggery's classroom ever, ever, EVER AGAIN!"

Fern was overjoyed. She smiled secretively at Howard and he smiled back. She and Howard were expelled! They'd never ever EVER step foot in this classroom again! She glanced at Lucess Brine, and there was that mixed expression again. Part of her seemed victorious and the other quite regretful. Lucess's eyes looked a little wet at first, and then water rose up in them and tears plopped onto each cheek. "Run away!" Lucess mouthed. "Run away, Fern!" But this time it didn't seem like something mean to say. It seemed like an urgent plea. Fern wasn't sure how to take it. She wanted to tell Lucess that she didn't care one bit! She was free! But it was as if Lucess knew something Fern didn't.

Fern and Howard walked out behind Mrs. Fluggery, the small pony galloping wildly around their feet.

THE INVITATION DISCOVERED

FERN AND HOWARD WERE SITTING IN FRONT OF
Vice Principal Wattley's desk. Vice Principal Wattley
was brand-new. Anyone could tell that just by looking
at his bald head, which still had considerable shine. If
there are classes in vice principal school devoted to
shining up a bald head, as I suspect there are, then let
me tell you, Vice Principal Wattley did very well on his
head polishing classes: A+++. His head glowed so much
that he didn't even look like Vice Principal Wattley as
much as he looked like a gold trophy version of Vice
Principal Wattley.

The real, true, actual principal of the school, a
bony woman named Sneed, had been out of town at

an educators' convention for a number of years. Fern knew her from photographs, one of which was life-sized and propped in her office chair. Fern and Howard had spied it through her open office door, and thought it was odd.

The school ran through vice principals quickly, perhaps because of Principal Sneed's absence. The vice principals did all the work, but a propped-up photograph in a chair got all the glory. Vice Principal Wattley, however, seemed like he was prepared to stay. He'd decorated his office elaborately; he'd bought a souped-up wooden rolltop desk with carved lion's feet and flanked by potted ferns. There were so many ferns that the place had a transplanted jungle feel. Fern, herself, felt like a very small fern in a sea of ferns. Bookcases, yes, but they were filled with cardboard displays of books—the kind you see in discount furniture stores.

Vice Principal Wattley had already called and talked to Dorathea and the Bone, as well as the Drudgers. Those conversations had invigorated him. He had never expelled anyone before. He was trying to sound grim, but he was truly breathless with joy. "This is what I've been preparing for! Expulsion! And now the time has come!" He had that aggressive air about him like a new bagger at the grocery store checkout, how they tend to pounce, crying, "Plastic or paper?" Fern had the sense that he was really feeling it—the vice principal vibe.

Fern and Howard were relieved to never be allowed to step foot in Mrs. Fluggery's classroom ever again. But Dorathea and the Bone were on their way to pick them up. They would drive them back to Dorathea's boardinghouse, where they would wait for the Drudgers—who were at an actuarial conference, assessing insurance premiums—and would come as soon as they could, though it might be late. "They have a schedule to adhere to," Vice Principal Wattley said, and Fern knew it was a direct quote. The Drudgers loved adhering to schedules. What would the Drudgers have to say? Would they understand at all?

Mrs. Fluggery was swimming through the ceiling-hung ferns around Wattley's desk. She was ranting and huffing and flapping. "Tell the parents that they're beastly children! Chigger bites! Hampsterheads!" Finally she ran out of steam. She had flopped into a fern-hidden armchair by the window and had only a little flap left in her. "Tell them about the violent pony! Tell them that I was nearly killed! Tell them, tell . . . them."

Vice Principal Wattley gave a frustrated sigh. He didn't believe in the violent pony part of Mrs. Fluggery's story, even though he should have! The pony, hidden in the pocket of Fern's hooded sweatshirt, was tired now too, but what if it began bucking wildly? Fern was very nervous.

Vice Principal Wattley was saying, "This is serious business . . . Indeed, indeed! But I am in charge, in full charge!" He repeated all this with relish.

Howard leaned over to Fern. "Stop it," he said.

"Stop what?" Fern asked.

"Stop humming! You shouldn't be so happy about this!"

"I'm not humming!" Fern said, but now she could hear the humming too. Where was it coming from?

Howard pointed to Fern's pocket, not the one with the pony in it. No, the pony wasn't humming. It was the other pocket. Why was her pocket humming? Fern clamped a hand over the pocket. She could feel the sharp edges of something shaped like a square. She didn't remember having anything in her pocket. Was it another apology from Lucess? No, it was too thick and pointy.

Vice Principal Wattley pushed a button on his desk intercom and asked his secretary, the wiry Mr. Ingly, to take Mrs. Fluggery to the nurse's office. "And roll the projector down to her classroom. Show them the inspirational film about the woman with no arms."

Fern loved that film. She'd seen it a bunch of times at

her old school. It always meant that the teacher was out, and it was quite good. The armless woman could trim her kids' hair with scissors in her toes. Fern loved the woman because she had so much going against her, but she wasn't doing things the way we'd expect. She was herself, and miraculous in her own very specific way. (It was the kind of inspirational film that was not shown to the students of my school, the Alton School for the Remarkably Giftless, because it would only have given us hope, and the administration figured: What was the point of that? We were too mediocre to have aspirations.)

Mr. Ingly shuffled through the ferns and took Mrs. Fluggery by the arm. They shuffled out together, Mrs. Fluggery still huffing, "Doily-, doily-, doily-brains."

Once the door shut behind them, Vice Principal Wattley said, "Obviously you two have put a strain on Mrs. Fluggery's logical mind."

They nodded. Fern patted the little pony in her pocket. *Don't wake up*, she said to herself. *Don't wake up, little pony!* She was afraid that if the pony caught Vice Principal Wattley's attention, he would confiscate it. Did I mention the enormous steamer trunk under the window filled with the collection of things that Vice Principal Wattley had confiscated in his short time at this school? Its lid was propped up, in a showy fashion. Fern could see two baseball mitts and a clarinet and a pair of crutches. Had he confiscated someone's crutches?

She also kept a firm grip on the other pocket, which was now leaking a hum.

"Expelled!" Vice Principal Wattley said, rubbing his hands together greedily. He opened his filing cabinet with a small silver key and rummaged through alphabetical files. "Erasers, evildoers, exams, expletives, expulsions! Here it is. The paperwork: expulsions!"

Fern had heard the word "expel" in a number of forms, but not this one: expulsion. It sounded much more awful, as if someone had mixed in the word *repulsion* to come up with something devilishly new.

Was the humming getting louder?

"I didn't get to expel children while on the old paper-folding circuit. Never. No, no, you had to be *nice* to the kids. You had to be *entertaining*."

"What's the old paper-folding circuit?" Fern spoke loudly to drown out the humming.

"I used to have a different job. I was on the circuit— you know, birthday parties, Easter egg hunts," Vice Principal Wattley said. He threw one hand in the air and swirled it. "I was an artist."

"Really?" Howard said, sounding a little too surprised.

"Is that so hard to believe?" He shoved two sheets of papers at Fern and Howard. "Sign here and here."

"No, no, not hard to believe," Fern said nervously. The humming was very distinct now. "I bet you were a great artist. What kind of art did you do?"

"Spontaneous Inspired Abstract Speed Origami."
Vice Principal Wattley cocked his head. "Do you hear
something?"

Fern ignored the question. "Origami? Like folding
pieces of paper into swans?"

"Swans!" Vice Principal Wattley was evidently dis-
gusted by swans. "The kids always wanted swans and
poodles and kitties. I was an artist! My work was
abstract! They just couldn't wrap their heads around
it!" He paused again. "I hear humming. Are you humming?" He stared at Fern.

"No," Fern said. "I'm not humming."

He looked at Howard.

"I'm not either. I don't even know how to hum."

"You'd better not be humming! You'd better be mis-
erable! You're being expelled and I'm the one expelling
you." He smiled proudly, looking off into the distance.
"Who would have guessed that I'd be here? Vice
Principal Wattley." He snatched the papers back, signed
them in a huge looping scrawl that took up most of the
page, and then he briskly picked up both papers and
folded, twisted, mangled, churned, curled, nibbled until
he was done, and the papers had taken on odd shapes.

"Swans?" Fern asked.

"Poodles?" Howard asked.

"No. The heart of a young man who has lost his art.

Sorry," said Vice Principal Wattley, suddenly very sad, as if to say you can take the boy out of the Abstract Origami circuit, but you can't take the Abstract Origami circuit out of the boy. "Bad habit," he said. He turned away from them in his swivel chair. "Out!" he shouted. "Wait out in the lobby! Go! Leave me alone!"

And so Fern and Howard took their expulsion papers and made their way out through the ferns. They walked past Principal Sneed's office with its life-sized photo staring out at them, and they sat down in the empty lobby, where Fern's backpack and Howard's briefcase were waiting. Mr. Ingly was gone, perhaps setting up the film projector. And so Howard and Fern were alone—well, aside from the sleeping pony and the hum coming from Fern's pocket.

"What is it?" Howard asked. "What's humming?"

Fern opened her pocket and pulled out a cream-colored square envelope. It had Fern's name printed on it in small gold curlicue letters and gold edging. "It's for me." She ran her fingers over the lettering. "It's really fancy. I don't know where it came from. Or why it's humming."

"It looks like an invitation," Howard said.

Fern ripped open the seal. The humming stopped. Fern read the invitation aloud:

"You are cordially invited to the
Annual Anybodies Convention
as the special guest
of the Secret Society of Somebodies
(The Triple S).
Please join us for our
formal meeting:
Midnight
Convention Day Two
after the motivational speech
by
Ubuleen Heet
(Founder of the Triple S).
Secret location to be revealed.
Be there or else!!!
Don't tell a soul."

"They should have put that last line first," Howard said. "Don't you think?"

"The Secret Society of Somebodies?" Fern said. *What would Lucess think of that, huh?* Ubuleen Heet? Who's that? Fern was giddy. This seemed like a royal invitation.

"I just think that if you don't want someone to read something out loud, you should say so up front. Right? And I don't like that 'or else' part. Or else what? It sounds awful! Doomed!"

Fern turned to Howard. "Is that all you can think about? I mean, it's mysterious! It's fancy! It has gold lettering and trim! It has a secret location to be revealed!" Fern didn't want to say anything about it, but this seemed like the first really royal thing to happen to her—an invitation to a secret society written on a fancy invitation! "I've never been invited to anything like this ever before!"

"I still haven't," Howard said.

"It's for the convention," Fern said.

"What convention?"

Fern stared at Howard. Sure, he didn't have access to *The Art of Being Anybody* like she did, but sometimes it amazed her how little he knew, or even wanted to know, about Anybodies. "The Annual Anybodies Convention," Fern explained. "It's in the city beneath the city."

"They *really* should have put that last line first. I

55

don't need any more information. The city beneath the city? Never heard of it and I don't want to," Howard said.

Fern shut the invitation, knowing she wouldn't ever make it to the convention, much less to the meeting with the secret location to be revealed. "I can't accept it anyway. I'm not allowed to go to the convention. Dorathea won't let me."

"You should have thrown it out. Just throw it out now. Pretend you never read the words 'or else,'" Howard said.

Fern didn't want to throw it out. "I think I'll hold on to it. Don't want it to fall into the wrong hands."

"Humph," Howard said.

"Don't tell a soul," Fern said. "Promise?"

"Humph," Howard said again. "It's trouble. I can tell. More trouble."

"But you promise?"

He nodded.

Just then the door opened. Dorathea and the Bone bounded in. They looked alarmed and bewildered. And in that moment right before they bombarded Fern and Howard with questions, Fern heard the tune in her head: up and up and down down down. Up and up and down down down. It was a dark song, Fern thought. It was unsettling the way it had worked its way into her head, and now she couldn't shake it.

5

WHISPERS . . . AND ANSWERS?

THE BONE'S CAR, AN ARTHRITIC JALOPY, WAS noisy. It shivered as it rode along. It moaned for no reason. The engine, a wheezy growler, always sounded like it was about to give up completely. And so even though no one was speaking at first, the car was far from silent.

It was all a little hard for Dorathea and the Bone to take—Fern and Howard expelled. Everyone was just letting it sink in—the blank future, the *what now?* They were all taking stock of the situation. (Sometimes I do that myself nowadays. Was I once a giftless boy who played the turkey in the Thanksgiving pageant—not a role that is as glamorous as it sounds, as the turkey always gets eaten in the end? And how did I become this enigmatic author, disguised as a Gypsy fishmonger just so that I can walk to the corner and buy a new electric toothbrush?)

Fern and Howard sat in the backseat, the pony in one of Fern's pockets, the invitation in the other. They both had their Abstract Origami expulsion papers on their laps. Fern stared at hers. She squinted. It didn't look like a young man who'd lost his art. It didn't look like much at all. Dorathea was squinting out her window. The Bone kept his eyes on the dusty road.

Dorathea broke the silence. "Take it from the top. What really happened?"

Howard and Fern took turns telling the story. They explained how Lucess Brine had started it all with a pinch in Fern's back, and how Howard had tried to help and how Fern had turned Mrs. Fluggery's hair into a small pony, which Fern took out of her pocket and held up for everyone to see.

The pony frisked its mane and whinnied.

"But actually I saved Mrs. Fluggery's life. I didn't try to kill her."

Fern was finished telling the story. Howard nodded secretively toward Fern's pocket where the invitation was.

Fern shook her head no. She would have liked to tell Dorathea everything—the humming, the gold trim, the name Ubuleen Heet, the Triple S, and the secret meeting place to be revealed. But she was afraid that Dorathea would take the invitation away, and although Fern was sure that she wouldn't ever accept, she still wasn't willing to give up the temptation.

"Well," Dorathea said, "I think you handled yourselves very well."

Fern sighed. This made her feel a little better.

"But we got expelled," Howard said.

"It goes that way sometimes," the Bone said. "But if you think about it, you two worked together. You did your best."

Fern was relieved. She could tell that Howard was too. He wasn't petting the pony quite so strenuously. She had a burning question, however. She opened her hand and looked at the name she'd written there the night before: Merton Gretel. She decided to try to steer the conversation toward him. "It was nice to have Howard there with me. He's like a brother now."

Howard looked over at her, a little shocked. They'd been through a lot, sure; and it was true, sure; but it wasn't the kind of thing that either of them said out loud.

"I never had a brother. The Miser is as close as I've come," the Bone said. "It's a nice thing. I miss him." The Miser and his friend the big-game hunter Good Old Bixie had gone out in search of adventure. This was very good for the Miser, who'd lost much of his boldness and was in need of adventure. They were sailing one of the peach-pit boats that the Bone and the Miser had made that past summer. The Bone looked wistful. "They'll be back at some point with good tales to tell."

Dorathea was quiet. Fern wondered if she'd say a word or if she'd just let the moment pass. But Dorathea let out a sigh. "I miss my younger brother. I don't like to talk about it."

"Why not?" Fern asked.

"Because I should have saved him. That's why."

"Stop," the Bone said gently. Obviously he knew the story. "Don't be so hard on yourself. You saved so many. And he knew. He did what he could in setting her up."

"Setting up who?" Howard asked.

"He helped take down the Blue Queen," the Bone said.

"This was years ago," Dorathea said. "There are hard things about being royal, Fern."

"What do you mean?" Fern asked.

Dorathea cleared her throat as if she'd lost her voice for a second. "I mean that there was a moment a long time ago in my fight with evil when I had the chance to save my brother or stop evil for the greater good."

"What did you do?" Fern asked.

"I stopped evil. I chose to protect all of the Anybodies."

"How?"

"My brother was married to the Blue Queen, and when he recognized her lust for power, he agreed to help stop her. He set up a time when she would be at ease, her defenses down, when we could easily attack her without hurting her. She was pregnant at the time, you see, with her first, and I knew that the plan put my brother in danger."

"He knew that too," the Bone said gently. "He knew the risks."

"What happened?" Fern asked.

"He disappeared. And the day after the battle, my brother's name was on the list of those she'd killed. . . . It isn't the crown and scepter that make you royal."

"What is it?" Fern asked.

"I've had to find my answers for myself, and you'll have to find your answers for yourself."

Fern didn't want to have to go looking for answers. Why couldn't being royalty be as simple as the crown and scepter? It was hers. She had it. Why couldn't that be the end of it?

"What's the Blue Queen like?" she asked.

"She was a number of years ahead of your mother in

school," Dorathea said. "She was the kind of kid who didn't have much going for her, but then I remember once she won an election for class recorder or something like that, and they gave her a ribbon that someone pinned to her lapel, and from that time on, she wanted more." Dorathea sighed. "Greed for power can start in the smallest ways and then just grow and grow. Just a little blue ribbon on a lapel. That's all."

"Merton was a good man," the Bone said. "A gentle soul. Gosh, I remember him at his wedding. He was so happy, this huge smile plastered on his face. But, well, she was already hungry for power then. She'd tried to run for mayor, but she didn't win. She probably already had her evil plan in store by then. She was faking it, I guess."

So Merton had married the Blue Queen without knowing what evil she was capable of. Fern felt sorry for him. She looked at the Abstract Origami expulsion papers and, for a moment, the papers looked sad, distraught, betrayed. *The heart of a young man who's lost his love.* That's what came to Fern. Merton had loved the Blue Queen. And had she loved him, too? What had gone wrong?

"I feel a little more sad this time of year. The anniversary of his death is coming up. Anniversaries are strange things," Dorathea said.

"For Anybodies especially," the Bone added.

"How are they strange?" Fern asked.

"An anniversary is when you remember the past event. In a way, the past is brought back. During anniversaries there's a certain weakness and, well, it forms an opportunity for the past to be brought back in a more real way. You know, for Anybodies it's easier on an anniversary to have the *idea* of the past come back as something *real*. Sometimes this is a good thing and sometimes it's a bad thing. And sometimes both."

Fern thought of the date that Merton died, the date when the Blue Queen lost her powers and the date that the invitation in her pocket would fall on. All the same day. Fern was putting it together. If the Blue Queen wanted to come back, she could use the souls of books for power, and she could pick the anniversary of her reign because on the anniversary it would be easier for the past to be not only remembered but brought back. The Blue Queen was planning on winning this time around. She wanted to rewrite history. "You defeated the Blue Queen," Fern said. "Can I ask the time of day?"

Dorathea looked at her granddaughter in the rearview mirror. Fern knew that her grandmother was on to the fact that Fern's mind was churning. "A little after midnight," Dorathea said. "And it wasn't easy."

Fern patted the invitation in her pocket, the meeting

time at midnight. The invitation was related to all this. It was a piece of the puzzle, but Fern wasn't sure how it fit. She knew why she hadn't thrown the invitation out. She knew that she was going to accept. She had to. She wasn't sure when or how it would happen, but she knew it was her destiny. There was no way around it.

"Sometimes I still talk to him," Dorathea said. "Merton."

"How is that?" Fern asked, tipping forward in her seat.

"I shut my eyes and cup my hands together like I'm whispering in his ear, like we're kids again and I've got a secret."

"Does he answer?" Fern asked.

"Not as a voice in my ear. But he answers," Dorathea said. "He does in his way."

EMERGENCY MEETING

WHEN THEY PULLED IN TO THE BOARDINGHOUSE
driveway, passing some talking crows and the hobbit
mounds, the Bone said, "Now we wait for the
Drudgers. You two should go straight to Fern's room
and reflect on the day. There's a lot to unravel, a lot to
learn."

The day's events were swirling in Fern's mind so furi-
ously that she wasn't sure what she'd learn from it all.

"What's going to happen next?" Howard asked.

"I don't know," Dorathea said. "I just don't know.
Go on now."

Fern and Howard walked quickly into the house,
happy not to have to talk to the Drudgers just yet. The

Drudgers, they knew, would be terrified by the rantings of Mrs. Fluggery. They would think there was some truth in all the hysteria. They disliked hysteria and rantings, and being terrified only made them more terrified.

Fern and Howard walked up to Fern's room. They propped their chins on their elbows and perched at the small grate covering the heating vent, where they'd be able to hear the conversation in the living room when the Drudgers showed up. They were quiet, both thinking their own thoughts. Next to them on the floor were their Abstract Origami expulsion papers. Fern was watching the miniature pony, its fur the skim-milky color of Mrs. Fluggery's hair. The pony was nosing the nubs of the throw rug, nudging Fern's backpack with its long muzzle. Every once in a while Fern would put her hand in her pocket just to make sure the invitation was still there. What was the Secret Society of Somebodies? And who was its founder, Ubuleen Heet? Fern glanced at the fish in the pond often. Frozen in place, its sad eye was on her.

She pulled out *The Art of Being Anybody* to see if any more had been written about them. She turned to the page with the entry *Fern Battles the Blue Queen*. There was a full sentence now. It gave a date—that day's date. Fern read on silently: *Fern and Howard, without his full will and desire, swam, thitherly, through an Invitation.*

There it was in black and white. Fern looked at Howard. He was slouched against the wall, worn down, exhausted, his briefcase flopped down beside him. He popped a breath mint and chewed. Should she tell him that the adventure was just beginning? That they were going to swim through an invitation, and do battle tomorrow at midnight? No, she thought to herself, it would only make him anxious. She knew that he'd be able to handle it when it came; no need to rile him now.

She pulled out the foldout map. She couldn't resist. She let it cover her knees and gazed at its winding streets. Dorathea came up with two bowls of soup and glasses of milk. They ate quietly. It grew dark. And finally there was the sound of a car in the driveway.

"They're here!" Howard said.

The two kids raced to the window. There were the Drudgers. They sat stiffly in their beige car, waiting there for a moment—bracing themselves?—the windows closed.

Eventually they walked through the yard. There was a series of short knocks. The door squeaked open on its hinges. The talking started up. Fern and Howard jockeyed for position over the vent. But the heat was on, blowing hot air in their faces, and it was impossible to hear a thing.

"I thought you said we'd be able to hear everything," Howard said.

"It'll click off."

More waiting. Fern was anxious now. Howard was too. They sat there poised and restless. Howard checked his wristwatch.

Then the heater clicked off with a moan, and Fern put on her sweatshirt. The kids could hear the voices, at least faintly. The Drudgers were talking about work.

"The actuarial committee was still going. We've missed out on a lot of insurance discussions because of this, and we won't be able to get those insurance discussions back," Mr. Drudger was saying, obviously shaken.

"We don't like things to disrupt our schedule," Mrs. Drudger said anxiously. "We don't like surprises of any kind, and especially not an awful surprise!" This was true. Once upon a time, they'd both been the kind of children who disliked Halloween because it makes everyone so fond of saying "Boo!" The kind of children to hide a jack-in-the-box in the back of a closet. The kind of children who never, not once, asked a trucker on the highway to blow his horn with that fist-pumping motion, because truckers and their horns are so unpredictable.

Howard looked at Fern warmly. "Aren't they the best?"

"Shh!" Fern said. "Listen."

"We are concerned," Mr. Drudger said, "about the welfare of these two children."

"The kids are fine. I mean, this isn't the best situation, but they were doing the best they could. Good kids, after all," the Bone said.

"Of course they're good kids, Bone," Dorathea said. "I'm sure that Mr. and Mrs. Drudger aren't suggesting that they're bad kids." But the way she said this made Fern think that was exactly what Mr. and Mrs. Drudger had been suggesting in the part of the conversation they'd missed due to the heater.

"When the vice principal called," Mr. Drudger went on, "we could hear that poor woman, Mrs. Fluggery, screaming about how they'd attacked her with a small, violent horse. Is that what good children do to their teachers?"

"It was a pony," the Bone corrected.

"And what will it be next time, Mr. Bone?" Mrs. Drudger asked. "An alligator? A shark?"

"These children need restraint. They need a controlled environment. We can't wait on this any longer," Mr. Drudger said.

"What kind of controlled environment are you thinking about?" Dorathea asked.

"Gravers Military Academy," Mr. Drudger said.

Fern and Howard both reared away from the heating grate, stirring the Abstract Origami expulsion papers. The pony let out a wild whinny. Fern felt sick. Gravers Military Academy! I once disguised myself as a cadet of no particular academy and, while just minding my own business, walking down the street, was mistaken for a runaway cadet and was sent back to a military academy that will go unnamed. I lived there for seven months until the whole mess was straightened out. So, I can tell you, Fern and Howard had every reason to be terrified. I still sometimes wake up in the morning and find myself saluting.

The idea of visiting the city beneath the city seemed farther away than ever. Was *The Art of Being Anybody* wrong? Fern folded up the large leathery map, one corner at a time. The rotund mosque gone, Bing Chubb's Ballpark gone, Willy Fattler's Underground Hotel gone. Finally it was all gone, even the castle's dirty bell tower. The map was as small and flat as an empty pocket.

Fern looked at Howard. Howard looked at her.

"I can't go to a military academy!" Howard said.

They both edged back to the heating grate.

"We've already made the call. We will be driving Howard there immediately. The program is for both boys and girls. They have a spot for Fern as well."

"You're joking," the Bone said. "Howard isn't military. Howard is Howard. He likes to sit around and read math books and be, well, Howard."

"And Fern! Ha!" Dorathea said. "She couldn't possibly!"

Fern paced. The invitation chose that moment to start humming softly again. She pulled it out of her pocket. She looked at her palm. Merton Gretel. She thought of dead books and the Blue Queen. She wouldn't be going to a military academy. She was going to the city beneath the city. This was it. This was the moment she'd been waiting for.

Mr. and Mrs. Drudger were silent. There was only the sound of shuffling papers. "Court orders," Mrs. Drudger said.

"Court orders?" Howard whispered.

"What?" the Bone said loudly.

"We've got the necessary paperwork," Mr. Drudger

said, as if that cleared everything up.

"You've got to do something!" Howard said. "Figure something out, Fern! We don't have much time!"

Fern was staring at the invitation. She couldn't help but think that it wanted an answer, and now she knew what the answer would be.

"What are you doing with that thing?" Howard was alarmed. "Put it away! It's no good."

Fern couldn't put it away. This was her destiny. She belonged at the convention—it was written in the book. She would battle the Blue Queen.

As soon as Fern had this thought, she felt a tug toward the envelope. The envelope popped open. Fern stared into it, the invitation in her hand. She felt another tug forward, and the envelope grew wider, big enough for shipping a fat book.

"Look, Howard," Fern said.

"What?"

"The envelope is growing."

Howard stared at it. "We need a plan! Not a growing envelope. I don't have time for any weird stuff now!" Howard was beside himself. Fern heard a slap of water. The toothy goldfish was swimming around in the painting now, the white lily pad flowers swaying over its head. The fish seemed to be urging her toward something with its unblinking glare, or warning her against something—Fern couldn't tell. The fish seemed to know her; she could sense it. It wanted to tell her something.

The conversation downstairs continued. "Fern is our daughter by law. You haven't adopted her. And I've proven that Howard is our biological son," Mrs. Drudger said. "We've begun the guardian process."

"But," Dorathea said. "But, but, Fern belongs here with us."

"Here?" Mrs. Drudger said. "With all these stuffy books, with all these dangerous creatures and these awful habits? Fern has become a menace over the course of one short summer. She's gone from straight-A student with us, to being expelled. She's out of control!"

"The court is on our side," Mr. Drudger said. "We're doing this for the children's own good."

But Fern wanted to tell them that she wasn't a menace. She'd been invited to attend the meeting of the Secret Society of Somebodies—maybe they would help her defeat the Blue Queen— and the more she thought about all this, the more she felt pulled toward the envelope, which was now the size of a plastic baby pool.

Howard couldn't deny the weirdness anymore. "What do you think it means?"

Fern was being pulled so hard now toward the envelope that she was swaying. "It's an invitation," Fern said. "It wants me to accept. It wants me, I think!"

"Do you want to accept?"

"I do." Fern felt a strong pull forward. Just then she heard her grandmother's voice below, and she knew that Dorathea would be disappointed in her. She'd told her that she couldn't go. Fern didn't want to defy her. "I'm scared. It might not be the right thing to do." The pull loosened its grip, and Fern wobbled backward. "I think it's letting me decide."

"Don't leave me here, Fern! Don't go!"

Mr. Drudger's angry voice rang up through the heating grate. "Well, we'll just go up and get them ourselves." Fern could hear the Bone and Dorathea saying, "No, no, no!" And then there were footsteps on the stairs.

Howard yelled, "They're coming!"

"I've got to do it," Fern said. "And you'll have to come with me, Howard."

"Where?"

"Into the envelope. Take my hand!"

"No," Howard said. "I can't. I don't want to. I'm too scared, Fern. Don't make me."

"C'mon," she said. She held tight to the growing envelope with one hand and reached for Howard with the other.

The fish was going wild, leaping and twisting. It

jumped out of the water and chomped a white lily pad flower. Petals flew out of the painting and drifted to the floor. Was the fish angry? Did it want her attention?

There was a sharp knock on the door.

Howard shook his head.

"Grab that book!" Fern shouted, pointing at *The Art of Being Anybody* on the bed. Howard was making a weird whine in his throat, an agitated and terrified whimper. But he grabbed *The Art of Being Anybody* and held on to Fern's arm with both his hands. The door to the bedroom flew open. Fern saw the Abstract Origami expulsion papers gust up, all fluttery for a moment. And then she looked up into the astonished faces of Mr. and Mrs. Drudger. "What in the world?" Mrs. Drudger said, pointing at the enormous envelope.

Dorathea and the Bone charged up behind them. Dorathea's mouth was a shocked "O."

The Bone said, "What in the—"

"I'm sorry," Fern said.

"My, my!" said Mrs. Drudger. Although that doesn't sound terrified, it was as strong as Mrs. Drudger's language got.

Mr. Drudger, not usually a man of action, lunged for Howard, but he was too late.

Howard shut his eyes tight as Fern shouted out, "I

75

accept your invitation!"

And with that, Fern and Howard were yanked into the envelope, which seemed to open up in front of them bigger and bigger. They seemed to be falling into and then out the other side of it, where they landed on a hard floor. It was dark.

In Fern's bedroom, Mr. and Mrs. Drudger, Dorathea and the Bone watched the envelope shrink back to its normal size. It froze in that shape for a moment or two, and then it shrank some more, until it wholly disappeared, and all that was left in its place was a handful of lily pad flower petals on the floor and a little tune that hung in the air for a moment. And then they, too, were gone.

The toothy goldfish swam into the depths of the painting. If anyone had noticed, they'd have seen his tail swishing—sadly?—away.

PART 2

THE CITY
BENEATH THE CITY

1

CHARLIE HORSE

LET'S BEGIN HERE WITH AN ELEVATOR OPERATOR.
Why an elevator operator? Well, because Fern and
Howard (and the miniature pony, now safe again in
Fern's pocket) had fallen through a hatch at the bottom
of the envelope that was attached to a hatch at the top
of an elevator—a glass elevator—and they landed on
the elevator's floor. On the other side of the glass, on
every side and below, was dirt.

It isn't easy to imagine, I know, falling through
hatches in swollen envelopes into glass elevators, but I
have complete faith in you, because you have a wildly
vivid imagination. (For example, the wildly vivid imagination of Missy in Hoboken; the strong, smart, and

bold perceptions of Chantelle from Girls Inc.; and the mazelike mind of Sister John Elizabeth, principal of Mount Aviat Academy! Stick with me now!)

Fern wondered if the glass elevator could fly. She'd read a book about a boy and a candy factory owner who flew in one such elevator. She would have asked right away, but the elevator operator was frowny and stern and proper.

He didn't react to Fern and Howard falling through the hatch. He pretended this kind of thing happened all the time, and it did. He was a formal man in a black cap who sat on a little black chair next to the automatic doors. A row of shiny buttons lined his vest, and they were under pressure, these buttons. The buttonholes were stretched so tightly, they puckered. The thread holding each button was exposed and frayed by the strain. The buttons stood out like a row bulging guppy eyes. The buttons were menacing, dangerous, like little pop guns all ready to go off.

The elevator operator simply said, "Floor, please!" in a way that made it seem like he wanted some flooring—tile, linoleum, fake hardwood—and he was going to be demanding about it.

"Floor?" Howard asked Fern. "Please?"

They were standing up now, brushing themselves off. Fern checked on the pony who, luckily, hadn't gotten crushed. There was elevator music, something sleepy and tinkling. But it wasn't very loud, and Fern and Howard could hear the gasps and muffled rantings of Dorathea, the Bone and the Drudgers overhead. Fern and Howard both looked up at the hatch, which had shut itself. Would the others find a way through to the elevator? Would they come after them?

"I think he wants to know what floor we want to go to," Fern whispered urgently to Howard.

"How do we know what floor?" Howard whispered back. He pointed at the hatch. "We've got to get out of here!"

Fern turned to the elevator operator. "We've been invited. We've come, um, through an invitation." She squinted at him, fearful that one of his buttons, trembling with pressure, might pop off and put out her eye.

The elevator operator glared at Fern, squinting away as she was. Evidently she wasn't the first person to fear his buttons.

"I know why you're doing that with your eyes. You think my buttons are going to blow! You think I'm too fat!" He let his fingers ruffle down the buttons. "Well, they do blow occasionally, but I fix them right up. I fix them right back into place."

The voices above were growing louder, and clearer, too. She could hear them arguing. Howard's and Fern's names were being tossed around angrily. Howard paced in a small circle, *The Art of Being Anybody* gripped under his arm.

"Where are we?" Howard was saying, looking at the dirt on the other side of the glass panes. "I don't understand. Are we underneath your bedroom? Are we downstairs? What's with the dirt? It doesn't make sense!"

The buttons were still irking Fern, however. She couldn't help but mutter the obvious questions. "Why do you fix the buttons, sir, if you don't mind me asking? Why don't you just get a bigger vest?"

"Code!" the elevator operator barked, rearranging his cap, angrily and for no apparent reason; the cap was just fine. "I'm union! This vest is to code. They don't come in bigger sizes. There's a maximum weight, you know! Can't take up too much weight! We're not like umpires!" He sighed sadly. "Lucky umpires."

Just then there was a *bing*, and the doors slid open,

revealing an elderly woman with a wire laundry basket on wheels in an apartment hallway.

"What is this?" Howard said, befuddled. He shoved his head out of the elevator and glanced up and down the hall.

"Sorry, Mrs. Hershbaum," the elevator operator said. "You'll have to leave the laundry behind. Already got two riders here, and as you know, I don't like to take on extra weight!"

"But I'm going to do my laundry at Melvin's! How can I leave my laundry behind?"

Melvin's? Fern knew the name of the place. It was on the foldout map of the city beneath the city. "Are we going to the city beneath the city?" Fern asked.

The elevator operator didn't answer Fern's question. He answered a question no one had asked, and that was: Why are you so afraid of taking on extra weight? (Elevator limits are usually two thousand pounds or more, and this elevator really wasn't close to that, even including Mrs. Hershbaum, a frail wisp of a woman, and her laundry.) "I had a bad elevator accident as a child," the elevator operator explained. "Too many people. An overload. I survived but was deeply scarred. So—"

"You became an elevator operator," said Mrs. Hershbaum wearily. "Shoulda gone into something closer to the ground!"

"Where'd she come from?" Howard popped his head back into the elevator and nearly screeched, "Is she underground? Is she in Dorathea's boardinghouse? Where did this hallway come from?"

"Well, sure, I'd have liked to have been an engineer! Who wouldn't? But I face my fear of elevators every day," the elevator operator said. "Sometimes I do get a little afraid, a little jangled nervousness about life, and at those moments, I eat a Twinkie or something, and that makes me feel safe and warm."

"Faced your fears! Ha! Can't even take a woman to the Laundromat!"

"I'm not taking you anywhere with that extra load! And that's final!" the elevator operator barked, and then he lowered his voice. "No can do!" He hit a button on the panel and the door hesitated long enough for Mrs. Hershbaum to show her displeasure with a grimace. The doors slid shut. Mrs. Hershbaum and her basket of laundry on wheels disappeared.

"We've come by invitation," Howard repeated nervously, looking at the dirt all around them. He had never been fond of oddness. "Does that mean anything?"

The elevator operator pulled a clipboard out from under his arm. "Name please!" Again, it seemed like he wanted Fern and Howard to name him instead of telling him their names. But they got the gist this time.

"Fern," Fern said.

"Howard," Howard said.

"Mmhm!" he said. He ran his finger down a list, paused, continued, paused, continued.

They could now make out the sound of shoes clipping around overhead. Howard whispered, "Hurry, hurry," under his breath.

Finally, the elevator operator shouted, "Six-oh-one!"

He pressed one of the unmarked buttons in a huge panel of unmarked buttons. Nothing happened. The music plinked on overhead. Howard and Fern shot each other anxious glances. They could hear Mr. Drudger stomping on the floor somewhere above them, saying, "Let's go about this logically. They can't be far away! They disappeared in this area."

"I wouldn't fool around there, Mr. Drudger," Dorathea was warning.

The Bone was calling, "Fern! Howard!"

"It doesn't make sense," Howard said, looking up. "How could they be there?"

The footsteps grew louder. Mrs. Drudger's voice was clear and close. "What's this, right here, in the spot where that thing shrunk and disappeared? Isn't it a latch?" There was some clicking. The hatch inside of the elevator jiggled.

The elevator operator wasn't flustered by the voices

or by the latch or by the elevator's lack of motion. "Are you ready?" he asked.

"Yes, yes!" Fern said. "What are you waiting for?"

"Just go!" Howard said.

"Is this your first time? I'll need to read a waiver. This isn't your ordinary elevator," he warned. "It's also a descendavator."

"Of course," Howard said. "All elevators are also descendavators! Just go!"

The latch was still twisting overhead.

"It's also a diagonavator, horizontavator, rapid-avator, vamoosavator."

"You made that last one up!" Howard shouted.

"I did not! I'm union! I'm up to code! Do you see this letter here from the elevator inspector?" The letter was framed in glass. "I run a tight ship!"

"Okay!" Howard said. "You run a tight ship! We're ready! Okay! So run it!"

"And you?" He looked at Fern.

Fern was staring at the hatch. "Ready!" she said.

The elevator operator calmly recited: "Keep all arms and legs inside of the elevator at all times. No screaming, yelling, or mocking of your elevator operator, who may be pushing his weight."

It was obvious he'd added this last line himself, but Fern didn't draw attention to it.

"That's all fine," Fern said.

"Yes, yes! We get it!" Howard cried.

The elevator operator smiled, just briefly. "Giddyap now, Charlie Horse!" he said. "Giddyap!"

Just at that moment, the overhead hatch opened. Mrs. Drudger's bland face appeared in the frame, the pale blue of the bedroom ceiling behind her like she was set against the sky.

"Oh, my!" she said.

And as the elevator (descendavator, diagonavator, horizontavator, rapidavator, vamoosavator) shot down with a violent burst of speed, the elevator operator's buttons began popping and pinging and ricocheting around. Fern and Howard squatted down and balled up, but they couldn't help but look back at what they were leaving behind. Four faces had collected there at the hatch: Mrs. Drudger, Mr. Drudger, the Bone and Dorathea—the paralyzed look of their shocked faces floating in an open square that grew smaller and smaller until Fern and Howard couldn't see them at all.

2

ELEVATORS APLENTY

FERN AND HOWARD WERE ON A REAL BUCKING bronco of an elevator. They careened madly through tunnels, around sharp corners and down chutes. The elevator dipped, spiraled and, once, looped. Fern's stomach looped right along, and Howard screamed like a wounded goat. They twisted, dawdled, then zipped, looped, zigged and, immediately thereafter, zagged. (There's a word for that but I'm too excited to think of it right now.)

Fern and Howard would sometimes try to get on their feet and surf, but mostly they were tossed and rolling on the floor, flattened against one pane of glass or another. Howard looked pale—prevomit pale. Fern was breathless and bruised.

The elevator was taking them deeper underground, and because it was glass, they could see everything flying past at great speed. It was shooting around roots and basements and gopher homes and square-bottomed swimming pools and lakes, close enough to the lakes to see the fish on the other side of their glass elevator. Fern didn't like to look at the fish, though. They reminded her too much of the menacing goldfish in the painting. She hoped she wouldn't see that fish again.

The elevator operator, his vest held together by one straining button and its suffering thread, never lost his balance. He never so much as bobbled. He sat on his chair, next to the panel of unmarked buttons—only one lit—and wore an expression of abject boredom. He tapped his foot lightly to the plinky music piped in through a speaker.

This was maddening to Howard. He glared at the elevator operator whenever he could, desperate for an explanation. When they hit a straightaway, he caught his breath and asked as many questions as he could fire off: "Where are we? How can this elevator exist in Dorathea's house and Mrs. Hershbaum's apartment building and by that lake? Don't people catch on—regular people? Where'd this elevator come from? Who manufactured it? How long has this elevator been in operation? And why don't you fall off your stool?"

Fern had only one question to add. It was the one she'd had the first time she saw the glass elevator. "Does this thing fly, by any chance?"

This caught the elevator operator's attention. He rearranged his black cap, patted it, then fiddled with his one remaining shiny button. "A History Lesson on the Anybody Elevator System. You have come to the right man!"

In precise detail and with great love and joy and a little nanny-nanny-know-it-all in his tone, he launched into an explanation. It went something like this:

"A ways back, a kid name Artie borrowed *Charlie and the Glass Elevator* from the library. Though he'd loved *Charlie and the Chocolate Factory*, this sequel didn't suit him. Artie thought it was a strange book that seemed like it was really about something else, but if you didn't know what that something else was, you were in trouble—an inside joke of a book. (May I interrupt to say I assure you that this book is about what it's about and not something else. So don't go wasting your time looking.) Artie liked the glass elevator, though, and he decided he was going to shake it out. It took fourteen days. He figured out how it worked, shook it back in very politely, and then designed glass elevators using a bit of hypnosis, transformation, and concentration. A great engineer! One of the best!" You could tell by the way he told the story that Artie was the elevator operator's hero as a kid. "He convinced Shirley Hurlman of Hurlman and Sisters to manufacture them in a factory in the city beneath the city. Hurlman designed the system of paths, a network that became worldwide: a fleet of hidden, highly disguised and thoroughly hypnotized elevators, trained to take you to the city beneath the city. Engineering," the elevator operator said dreamily. "If I didn't have to face my elevator fears day in and day out, I'd take classes."

Fern said, "You should take classes, if that's what you want."

"Don't be silly," the elevator operator said. He cleared his throat and went on with his telling. "The really great Anybodies can find the city beneath the city in their own ways," he explained. "But for the less gifted or those who don't want to waste their gifts on travel—and most fall into one or the other group—the elevators work best. In New York, for example, there are hidden elevators in various locations." He named a few: behind a certain bookcase at the Bank Street Bookstore; in the back room of Epstein's Bar; inside a certain Gap dressing room.

"These elevators will take you straight to a number of places in the city beneath the city: a spot near the concession stand at Bing Chubb's Ballpark; to the back of Melvin's Laundromat and Dry Cleaner's where the pressed shirts draped in plastic ride the carousel; or to the side door next to the jukebox at Jubber's Pork Rind Juke Joint; or up into the confessional of Blessed Holy Trinity Catholic Church and Bingo Hall.

"Regular people don't know that we exist, and they stick to that notion. It's easier than you'd think. The Anybodies philosophy, you see, depends on the idea that the world is in a constant state of change, and one of the things that changes most is a person's perception of things. Your perception, Howard, was that we were in part of a house. Mrs. Hershbaum's perception was that we were in her apartment building. Both were right enough." Here, he smiled as if he'd really made everything crystal clear. "So, you understand."

"Not at all!" Howard said.

"Humph," the elevator operator grunted. "Well, we're getting closer to New York now. Can you understand that?"

"Yes," Howard said, and then he stared out. They were flying past dirt. "Kinda." The elevator took a sharp left. Howard and Fern slammed into a wall. "But you didn't answer my question about why you don't fall off your stool!"

"I don't fall off my stool because I'm living in my perception, and in my perception, elevator operators don't roll around on the floor."

94

"What about my question?" Fern asked, trying to inch up the side of one of the glass walls.

"Well, sure it flies! Didn't you read the book?"

"Oh, no," Howard moaned. "No, no, no! It isn't mathematically, statistically . . . Well, it doesn't add up!" But even as he said these words, his voice shook with a lack of confidence. He knew that so many things weren't logical. He'd already dived through an envelope. Fern had a miniature pony in her pocket made out of his teacher's hair. The book that he was holding was filled with an entire art that was not sensible.

Soon the obstacles became more frequent, and the elevator was having to skinny in, and curve, as if it weren't made of glass for a moment but of something more flexible. This made Fern and Howard very nervous. The pony shook and pawed in Fern's pocket. They rode for a while alongside a subway car. Fern and Howard pressed their faces to the glass and waved, but the people on the other side didn't seem to notice. The ones that were looking in the right direction seemed to be staring only at their own shortsighted reflections in their subway windows, which isn't unlike New Yorkers. (Also, let's be honest. If some of those New Yorkers had seen two kids waving from a glass elevator traveling sideways beside their subway car, most of them would be too above-it-all to react. At most, they'd sigh, and say, *Oh, that again!*)

As they peeled away from the subway, taking a sharp left, the elevator maneuvered, herky-jerky, around all kinds of tubes and pipes made of cement and metal, taking them lower and lower. They even saw the hull of an old ship.

"We're going deeper underground," Howard said.

"We'll be there soon!" the elevator operator barked.

Moments later they popped out of the chute and found themselves in the air. The elevator relied on no ropes, no cables, no pulleys. The elevator operator had been right, after all. The glass elevator could fly.

"Here it is," the elevator operator announced. His remaining button was tense and quivering on his belly. "The city beneath the city."

"Oh, look," Howard said. "Just look!"

"I told you," Fern said, in awe of it all. "I told you!"

The city stretched out below them as they hovered and then plummeted toward it. The thick roots of New York City were exposed, and the city beneath the city grew around pipes and ductwork and abandoned chutes. Because of being underground, the city had to manufacture the sun. Everything glittered with artificial light—lanterns and neon signs and overhead lights like those in stadiums.

Hands pressed to the glass, Fern and Howard stood at the elevator's glass wall and stared out. They flew over Bing Chubb's Ballpark, where there was a late inning and a cheering crowd, and then up the courthouse row. Carved angels roosted around the church steeple. They circled the mosque, golden and shining, just once. There were other glass elevators too, bustling along, carrying Anybody families and business people, and occasionally a large glass elevator of heavy cargo— once, watermelons. Fern ran from one side of the elevator to the other.

"What are you looking for?" Howard asked.

"The castle." Fern lowered her voice so the elevator operator couldn't hear. "It's got to be here."

"What castle?"

"I'm royalty now, Howard, remember? The castle is, well, it belongs to the family. We should live there, Howard. We should live in the castle."

"We should? Me too?"

"Yes, sure. Beats military academy."

The elevator took a sharp right. They toppled in one direction and then righted themselves.

"Is that it?" Howard said, one finger pressed to the glass.

That's when Fern saw it. The castle. It was tall with many towers and a black grill gate with gold tips and surrounded by green shrubbery in a fancy design, the wide lawn with its grassy mound, a fishpond, and a gazebo, white and nearly glowing. There was the tall spire that Fern remembered so clearly from the book, and just as in the picture, the spire's tip was wedged into the dirty underside of Manhattan. But it was grander to see it in person, the way it sprawled and gleamed.

"Yes," Fern said. It was so grand that Fern imagined that the Blue Queen didn't need any other motive for her eleven-day reign other than just wanting to live in such a place. "Wouldn't you like to call that home?" Fern asked.

"Wow," Howard said.

Even the pony got to see it and let out an awed neigh.

Fern gazed at the castle. Its spire was barely visible in a small patch of fog. Fern wanted to tour the grounds, go inside, see if there was a throne, and if there was, maybe even sit on it. But then she caught herself. The Blue Queen was here, most likely, somewhere in this city, thinking her dark thoughts, hatching her evil plans, maybe eyeing the castle herself. Fern felt heat run through her body—a feeling of strength and pride. This was her destiny, her royal fate. She could feel the rightness of it all.

The elevator dropped into a square hole on a street corner, as if it were being sucked down. The pipes grew larger and louder. The chute around them became more dense and rocky. "I don't like this," Howard said.

"Me neither," Fern said.

Just when she thought they couldn't possibly go any deeper, they zipped back up again. The chute was dark, so they couldn't see where they were.

"Whoa, Charlie Horse!" the elevator operator called out. The elevator started to screech and shiver. Fern thought she smelled a fine whiff of something burning. *Brakes?* she wondered. The elevator slowed down, began stuttering. The elevator operator's final button snapped loose and ricocheted, pinging against all the walls, and then with a high-pitched whine, the elevator ground to a stop.

Fern and Howard and the miniature pony were dazed. From overhead, the elevator speaker plinked out a warped, warbling, exhausted song. And the shiny gold button rolled to a stop in the middle of the floor.

But when Fern and Howard looked up to see if it was now safe to stand, the elevator operator had a new row of polished buttons, highly pressurized, glinting down his vest.

THE BED BENEATH THE BED

THE ELEVATOR WAS WET WITH CONDENSATION
from the effort of the trip, and so the elevator operator
slipped off his stool and began wiping down the moist
walls with a small towel he'd pulled from his trouser
pocket. "Good old Charlie Horse. We survived another
one," he said. He looked nervous. "What's next? Where
will we be off to this time?"

Fern and Howard stood and slowly turned circles to
see where, exactly, they'd ended up. On the other side
of the glass door, there were six wood panels. And
looking through the glass walls to their left and right,
Fern and Howard saw fur—thick, glossy, brown fur—
which, I'm happy to report, did not seem to be attached

to live bears. It was simply fur. Behind them there was, of all the strangest things, what looked like snow, falling softly, and a distant light. "Where are we?" Fern asked, feeling like the place was strangely familiar.

"Six-oh-one," the elevator operator said. "Like the clipboard said."

"Six-oh-one?" Howard asked.

"Room Six-oh-one, of course," the elevator operator said. He was holding the towel and Fern noticed his hands were shaking. He was talking to himself now, looking off into the distant snow outside the elevator. "Who do you think will ring us next? Who do you think? Will we survive the next one?" He pulled a Twinkie out of his jacket pocket and unwrapped it quickly.

"I know this place," Fern said. "I feel like I've been here before."

"Here?" Howard was astounded. "We don't even really know where *here* is!" (Of course, I, N. E. Bode, your trusty narrator, know exactly where here is. I know exactly all the lovely and odd and scary things that lie before them. But they didn't, so let's not get ahead of ourselves.)

"I can't explain it, Howard. It's just how I feel. There's something about the fur and the snow and that light back there through the snow. And this, too, the wood."

"Well, I want to get out of here." And then Howard paused. "I think."

With that, the elevator operator hit a button. The pony was sitting up in Fern's pocket, its hooves hooked over the edge, looking around with its large eyes. Howard held the book and closed his eyes and waited. The elevator gave a weary *bing*, and the doors slid open. But the wood paneling was still blocking their way.

"Oh, sorry about that," the elevator operator said, his words muffled by a Twinkie. "You sure you want to go? I don't mind kids. They don't weigh as much. Less chance of, you know, disaster!" He opened a little hook on the wood paneling, and two doors swung away from each other. The miniature pony whinnied, and the sound bounced around the small room.

"I think we've got to go," Fern said. "You'll be okay."

"Will I?" the elevator operator asked, opening another Twinkie.

"I have a thing with sweets myself," Howard said. "Might want to lay off them."

Fern wanted to help the elevator operator, to say the right thing, but she wasn't sure what that right thing would be. He was a grown-up, she thought. Grown-ups should know how to take care of themselves. Fern wanted to take care of herself, for example. She wanted to prove that she could. She smiled. "You'll survive," Fern said, but that wasn't what she wanted to say, not exactly, and so she added, "You know, if your perception of an elevator operator is that one doesn't roll on the floor, why can't your perception of yourself change too?"

"I don't follow," the elevator operator said.

"Why don't you perceive yourself as the kind of person who doesn't have to prove that he's not afraid of elevators, and perceive yourself as an engineering student?"

"Why don't you?" the elevator operator said defensively.

"I don't want to be an engineering student; you do," she said.

The elevator operator stared at her hard. "I think you know what I mean," he said.

And Fern felt like he could see that she was on her own this time, that she couldn't rely on the Great Realdo, that her grandmother was getting older now. Was he telling her to perceive herself as more able, more ready for battle? "I just think it would help you, that's all, if you perceived yourself as you wanted to be. . . ," she said quietly.

The elevator operator smiled shyly, fiddled with his buttons. "I don't know why I don't do that," he said, lift-

ing his chin up. "I'm not sure. I could, I suppose. I could."

Fern and Howard stepped out of the elevator and through the wooden doors, and down a step onto wall-to-wall carpeting. The wooden doors shut behind them. They heard the elevator doors *bing*, and then the muffled voice of the elevator operator talking to Charlie Horse. "Giddyap! Let's go!"

The room was filled with a plush four-poster bed, a writing desk, a tiny refrigerator, a wall-hung mirror, a painting of a farmhouse. Room 601 was a hotel room. Fern whispered to herself, "Willy Fattler's Underground Hotel?" She turned around to see what they'd just stepped out of, exactly. She wasn't completely surprised to see that it was a wardrobe.

"I knew there was a reason I felt like I'd been there before," she said. The wardrobe is part of a book that's also about a lion and a witch. Fern knew the book quite well—so well, in fact, that it seemed like she'd really experienced it, which is why this had felt so familiar. (One day you might come across something that reminds you of this book—a certain teacher's hairdo, a certain vice principal's origami, a certain elevator operator's vest buttons—and you might have the very same familiar feeling. I certainly hope so.) "The fur was just from coats," she explained to Howard. "And the snow is in Narnia." It crossed Fern's mind to step into the wardrobe and have an adventure somewhere else, but Fern is Fern, and she belongs right here. She felt needed here. She was going to battle the Blue Queen.

Howard peered around the room. He coughed and patted down his mussed hair. "Hello?" he said softly. "Hello?" There was no answer. The room was empty. "Do you think this is somebody's room?" Howard asked. He pulled out his wallet and rummaged. "I can't pay for a hotel room," he said.

Fern ran to the bathroom. It was white and glistening. White fluffy towels sat in metal racks attached to the wall. There were miniboxes of soaps, minibottles of shampoo. When Fern lived with the Drudgers, they'd stayed in the hotel at Lost Lake, and because the lake was lost and the place was dismal, Fern had liked the minibottles of shampoo most of all. There was a little plastic circular container of shoe polish and a stack of toilet paper rolls. The toilet seat was wearing a paper sash that read SANITIZED FOR YOUR PROTECTION. She picked up one of the bottles and read it. "It's really true!" Fern said, bounding back into the room. "We're here! We've made it!"

She tossed the bottle to Howard, who dropped it, then picked it up off the floor and read it aloud: "'Compliments of Willy Fattler's Underground Hotel.' What does this mean?"

Just at that moment, a gauzy netting suddenly dropped from the ceiling and down over the bed, including Howard sitting on it. The room then groaned into unfinished wood and bamboo furnishings. It became more primitive. The wardrobe became a little leaning cupboard, and a large net of bananas grew from a knob on the wall. The telephone turned into a parrot. The wall-to-wall carpeting disappeared from one side of the room to the other, crumbling into dusty sand on a wood floor.

Howard had stopped breathing. "What?" he said weakly. "What happened?"

"It's Willy Fattler's! It's an Anybodies hotel! It's

always transforming! That's what! Isn't it great!"

"Not great!" Howard said, batting his way out from under the mosquito netting, shooing the parrot circling his head. "Not great!"

Fern ran to the front door of their room.

"What are you doing?" Howard asked.

"Taking a look!" she said. She turned the knob and opened the door just enough to poke her head out. The hallway was empty, lined with numbered doors. At first it seemed like a normal hallway in a normal hotel, but then the nubby oatmeal carpeting swirled into a Persian print, and the flowered wallpaper turned golden and satiny. "Imagine that!" she said.

"Let me see," Howard said.

Fern dipped lower so that he could peer out over her head. "Someone's coming."

They closed the door except for a small crack, and watched an elderly couple shuffle up to the room directly across from theirs.

"Ever-changing cocktails!" the old man said.

"Yes, but you didn't have to try them all, Gerald!" the old woman chided him.

Between the couple, Fern and Howard had a good view of the doorknob, which was gold then crystal then ancient-looking, and the old man's key changed three times too—from a card key to a key with a metal tag to an old black skeleton key—before he slipped it into his pocket.

"Did you see that?" Howard asked.

"Yep!" Fern said.

When they shut the door and turned back to the room, everything was Egyptian. The bed a gold sleigh with a pillow-stuffed mattress, hieroglyphics on the walls, a lot of asp and cat art.

"Don't you love it?"

"I prefer predictability, regular patterns. I like things to be reliable."

Fern grabbed *The Art of Being Anybody*. She flipped to the page with her entry. She read it quickly, looking for new information. There it was:

> . . . *Fern arrived withly Howard, in whole, at Willy Fattler's Underground Hotel, and withwhile in the City Beneath the City, they held slumber in an everchanging environ to prepare for the Battle with the Blue Queen at Midnight on Day Two of the convention.*

"What time is it?" she asked.

Howard checked his watch. "Just about midnight," he said. "Why?"

"Nothing," Fern said. They had twenty-four hours

before the battle. Only that. Why wasn't *The Art of Being Anybody* telling her what she needed to know? She decided she should follow its plan—*slumber in an everchanging environ*—here.

"We should slumber," she said.

"Slumber? How can you sleep on a bed that is going to turn into different beds all night long!"

"I don't think we should sleep on the bed," Fern said.

"You don't?"

"We can't. What if this isn't our room? What if someone comes to claim it in the middle of the night and finds us sleeping in it?" Fern said.

Fern climbed under the bed—a tall Victorian bed with lots of lace.

"A bed under the bed? In the city under the city?" Howard said quietly.

"It's better than getting caught," Fern said. "And kicked out onto the street."

Howard shrugged and joined her. He used *The Art of Being Anybody* as a hard pillow. They both wiggled to get comfortable. They could only really lie on their backs, but they both put their hands behind their heads and stared upward the way you would in a field, looking at stars—if you were the type of person comfortable with that kind of thing, which I'm not. With the pony curled between them, they gazed at the ever-changing bedsprings, which groaned in one direction and then a few minutes later in another. Dust ruffles at their sides came and went.

Howard promptly fell asleep, but Fern lay awake, thinking of the gold-trimmed invitation. Was the secret location of the meeting going to be revealed to her? How, exactly? When? She would battle the Blue Queen. That was all she could think about under an ever-changing bed in an ever-changing room in an ever-changing hotel in the city beneath the city.

DEAD BOOKS

WHEN FERN WOKE UP, SHE WAS SURPRISED TO find herself under a bed with a small pony nestled next to her. It took a minute for the day before to come clear. But once it did, she was surprised again to note that there was morning sun coming in through a window on one side, and a bright light on in the hotel room coming from the other side. Hadn't they only left on the bathroom light? She was surprised to see a slight dimple in the mattress above her—a dimple that didn't go away even as the bed changed from one kind to another. And even more surprising—or should I say alarming?—was the snoring. There were two snorers, to be exact: one light and puffy, the other one sickly and whistling, like a dying bird.

She put her hand over Howard's mouth and gave him a little shove. His eyes opened widely, and he jerked his head back and forth. Fern put her finger to her mouth and then pointed up to the mattress. His eyes went wild for a moment. Then he nodded, and she took her hand off his mouth.

Just then the dying-bird snore sputtered and turned into a rattling cough. A pair of feet appeared beside Howard's head. But they were only barely recognizable as feet. They seemed boneless, more like something that had slid up from the dirt. And they were white, a horribly pale, bloodless, ghostly white, like large, blind, albino slugs. (Are there such things?)

"Wake up. Wake up! Help me out of this bed!" It was a woman's voice, sickly, quavering, but with a cold and metallic tone.

"I'm up," a young girl responded.

Two slim feet, about the size of Fern's, swung to the floor beside the other pair. Fern took this moment to peek out in the other direction. She could only see the top of the night table, which was covered in a doily. It just had three objects on it: a tall, thin lamp with a dainty fringed shade, an old-fashioned telephone—the tall kind with the earpiece sitting in a cradle—and a large goldfish bowl with a large orange goldfish swimming circles inside. Did the goldfish have a darker orange spot under his one eye? Yes. Yes, it did. Fern shrank back under the bed.

The girl was walking the woman away from the bed.

"Did she arrive?" the girl asked.

"Do you see her?" the woman said harshly.

"Why hasn't she gotten here?"

"She'll come. The invitation was designed to bring her here, directly. Get dressed. Red, please. Wear the red dress."

Her invitation? Someone had designed it to bring her here directly? Were these two people part of the Secret Society of Somebodies? Fern still didn't know what that was. But she knew she didn't like the way they were talking about the whole thing, as if she were a package they were expecting in the mail. The pony still asleep, Fern and Howard listened to shuffling, water running, the flush of a toilet, the sounds of someone brushing teeth—the comings and goings of a morning routine. But through it all, the woman was barking at the girl.

"Like this!" she'd scream. "Stop it! Help me!" "Pay attention!" "Get my other shoes!"

Now the pale and boneless feet appeared again. Fern and Howard could see the girl's legs, kneeling beside the feet. Her hands worked hard to stuff the pale feet into a pair of high heels.

Fern could feel her back prickling. It was hot under the bed, stuffy and stifling. Fern wanted to grab hold of Howard's arm. She was scared. The hotel room had a sour smell and an electrified feeling of something gone very wrong.

"Help me to the vanity! I'm feeling weak again. Get the box over here!" the woman said.

The girl walked her away. And then walked back, dragging a box to the side of the bed. She reached inside and pulled out a stack of books. "Let's just have breakfast first," the girl said nervously. Her voice sounded slightly familiar, as if her voice were wearing a disguise—a nervous disguise.

"I don't need breakfast. You know that. Breakfast doesn't do me any good. Be of some use. These books aren't yet dead. I can still draw more from them."

Fern and Howard exchanged a look of fear. Dead books! She remembered the way Dorathea and the Bone had talked about them and about the Blue Queen. Was this the Blue Queen? Right here in Willy Fattler's hotel? Were they going to kill books?

Fern knew it was the Blue Queen. She knew because she could feel it. Even though the Blue Queen was too weak to get out of bed without help, too weak to put on her own shoes, there was something terrifying about her—the ghostly feet, the cold ring to her voice. She seemed to have a certain power, even in her weakness, like a coiled snake.

The girl brought over a stack of books. She was wearing white socks and shuffled her feet nervously.

The room grew dark as if it were suddenly dusk. The sour smell grew to a sour wind, old and medicinal and fog-thick. It rippled through the dust ruffle, making Fern think of the words "ether" and "poison gas" and "evil." Fern and Howard both covered their noses and mouths in the crooks of their arms. The pony woke up and buried his face in Fern's sweatshirt. The room seemed almost yellowish now, sickly. The wind churned, and the goldfish jerked and splashed in his bowl, sloshing water till it spilled onto the floor.

The Blue Queen began laughing. "Souls," she hissed. "I'll just take a bit. Just enough to get me through the day."

"Not too many," the girl said.

"I'm not foolish. I know that I need to save them for tonight."

And the wind grew so strong that the books on the floor tipped and began sliding toward her, their pages splayed open, rattling. Howard was on his side, watching. *The Art of Being Anybody*, which Howard had stuffed under a towel to make a bigger pillow, started to be dragged forward too. It bumped into Howard's back. Fern put a hand on it. Howard turned, grabbed it, and rolled on top of it. He looked frantic. Fern felt frantic too.

"That's enough," the girl shouted above the whipping wind. She bent down to grab some books, but she couldn't keep hold of them all. Fern and Howard could only see the girl's knees and fast-working hands. The books were gliding away from her, and things were being pulled from them. A glowing breath, a rising misty, sunlit cloud—they were hard to describe. But they were egg shaped, like airy, glistening eggs. The girl was desperately trying to keep them inside of the books. She kept shutting the covers as quickly as she could, but it was hard to keep up.

"Not too many!" the girl shouted. "You have to save them! Remember?"

"Let go of them! I need!" the Blue Queen shouted, as if she'd forgotten what she'd said before. "I need them!"

Fern knew somehow that she was watching the souls of books being lifted out of them. She was watching books die. The Blue Queen was unable to stop herself. She was supposed to be hoarding the souls—like Dorathea had guessed—but she couldn't stop. Fern could see the titles of a few of the books. Flipping past was a copy of a Terry Pratchett book with those nomes on the cover trying to steer a truck; that eerie book about a girl named Coraline; the book about the smiling dog that had made Fern cry; and then her heart skipped wildly, because she saw a book that she knew better than all the other books combined, a book with a picture of a girl on the cover, a girl with big eyes and a roosterlike lock of hair, a girl named Fern.

It was, of course, *The Anybodies* by, well, N. E. Bode. Me. And I can't speak for Terry Pratchett or Neil Gaiman or Kate DiCamillo on how it felt for them to have that bit of their souls that they'd stitched into their own books ripped out. No, I cannot. But I can tell you that I was in a donut shop at the moment (disguised as a hefty mobster), and although I didn't know what was happening, I felt something awful—as if a corner of my own soul, the one I walk around with day in and day out, went dark. I stumbled forward, like something alive in me had been snap-jerked out of my chest. Suddenly breathless, I leaned on the glass counter of the donut shop and wheezed, and stared at the glazed pastries without really even seeing the glazed pastries. The kid behind the counter asked if I was okay, and I said that I wasn't. He started to call the paramedics, because I was so blanched. "No, no," I told him, and I walked out of the donut shop and made my way dizzily onto the sidewalk.

And you have to keep in mind that every time a reader finishes a book that they love, they know the writer's soul. And so with each of the Blue Queen's swallows, all of the readers who'd poured themselves into each of these specific books could feel the loss. (That copy of *The Anybodies*, for example, had been borrowed by a girl named Hayley Twyman from Mr. Flom's fourth-grade classroom in Tallahassee and mistakenly left on a bus, where it was read by a girl from St. Bernadette's who took it on a field trip to the Philly Zoo, where it dropped from her bag in the monkey house and did some time in the lost and found until one of the employees took it home to her daughter Ursula, who shared it with her friend Trevor Hobbs, who took it on vacation to Manhattan Beach, where a beachcomber in from Boston stole it—a nice enough kid making bad choices—and feeling guilty for having stolen it, put it on the shelves of the Lizard's Tale, a bookshop outside of Boston, where a boy named Levi bought it and cherished it and took it everywhere he went—once namely to a certain spot near World's End in Hingham, where it was lost along with the backpack that it was in . . . Let's cut to the chase: eventually it ended up in the hands of an Anybody who brought it to the city beneath the city, where it was stolen by the Blue Queen for her evil purposes.) All those readers let out a sad sigh, right in the middle of what they were doing. It was a collective sigh that ran coast to coast. A gust of wind that stirred things up for a moment, maybe even created a little gustnado in China or somewhere. A loss. Not something they could name, but just a sense of something having been taken away.

Fern sighed too. Deeply. And then she scrambled down to the foot of the bed—hard to do since the bed at this moment was a low cot on old, sagging springs. She had to see what would happen to my soul next. Howard tried to grab her arm to stop her, but she slid along and peeked out from under the haggard cot.

The Blue Queen was breathing the souls in through her open mouth. Her lips grew redder, her cheeks so flushed they turned blue. In fact, all the veins that Fern could see glowed bright blue. Her throat seemed to expand with the intake of each bit of soul—Pratchett and Gaiman. She was going quickly from ghostly white and limp, to full, puffed, robust and blue. She swallowed and swallowed—DiCamillo and then Bode.

Fern was horrified. She felt sick, and that's when her hands began to flutter at her sides. She lifted them up. They were heavy and unwieldy. Howard glanced over and gasped. Fern's hands had become books—two open books with flapping pages. Howard raised his own heavy hands, bookish in weight—his fingers, too, turning into pages. Their hands were being pulled, just like the others—pulled toward the Blue Queen. Fern felt as if she were being ripped from herself. Her own soul, shimmering and lit, appeared in the books' pages. Howard reached over and shut her book-hands as fast as he could with his own. Fern slipped hers underneath her rump to keep them pinned shut. Howard followed her lead. Fern's soul stopped. It bumped against the shut covers of the books but couldn't escape. How? Fern thought. How had that happened? Howard was shaking, his eyes screwed shut.

By then the Blue Queen had eaten enough souls, but

she was still grasping each of the souls being drawn to her. Powerful and mighty from the consumption, she caught them and pressed them with her cupped hands till the glowing-egg souls were the size of egg-shaped pills. She was saving them, Fern realized, stockpiling souls for later. She put them into small jars that were already nearly filled with the same, compressed to a small glowing egg and popped into a jar—this bit of soul and the bit of soul after mine and the next soul and the next and on and on. The wind stopped. The sickly fog thinned. The room brightened again.

"That was too many!" the girl said, out of sight, her voice frantic.

"Soon I won't need books anymore! Oh, how much easier it will be to steal souls directly from the living! How much easier! And all at once, my dear. All at once!"

The girl sighed. She sounded tired, having chased the books, or maybe she was tired the same way Fern was, from having seen something awful. She wondered what the girl looked like, but Fern couldn't risk being seen. She tucked herself deeply under the bed.

The Blue Queen snapped at the girl. "Don't be weak. We're close. All that's left is to get the ivory key from Fattler. All I need is that key!"

The ivory key—a key to what? What would she have

broken into by now? Fern stared at the box springs, knowing that this, too, was very bad.

"I will get what I want! Do you hear me?"

"That hurts," the girl said. "I'll have a bruise there."

The woman's voice turned now. "Oh, princess," she said. "Oh, rightful princess, dear. Soon you won't have to be disguised, no, no. You won't have to hide in plain sight anymore! It will all be worth it in the end. You'll have what you deserve and want." Fern looked at Howard, and he looked back, wide-eyed and shaken. Fern felt sweaty all over, and now chilled. Rightful princess? Hide in plain sight?

"I've got a beautiful plan all laid out. This window of the anniversary of my defeat, I will take advantage of it, my dear. This time I will be victorious. I have enough power this go-around."

"What I want is my father back," the girl said.

"Don't be ridiculous! Most of poor Merton's soul is long gone. Poor, poor Merton!" Her voice didn't sound sympathetic, however. It seemed she hated Merton more than she felt sorry for him. "He doesn't have enough soul left to power a bigger human body. He's fine as he is. And he's still of use. He spied very well on Fern, spied quite nicely. Hand me my moth brooch! And I've got to powder my face so I don't look so ravenously blue."

He didn't have enough of his soul left? He was with them in a smaller form? He'd spied on Fern? Could it be that the girl's father—Fern's great-uncle Merton— was the goldfish who'd watched her from the painting? Was Merton Gretel alive—not dead at all, but alive in the form of a fish? He'd been alive all this time. Merton Gretel. The faint letters of the name were still legible on Fern's palm. She felt a hardening in her chest at the sound of that name spoken with that voice.

Fern could hear the Blue Queen clicking through a makeup bag. The girl knelt beside the bed and reached into a suitcase propped there. She pulled out a large, shiny, blackish-greenish brooch. She ran her thumb over it gently. Fern looked at the brooch carefully. It was made of ten shellacked cocoons, delicately spun—ten of them arranged around one center moth, with a shiny pin stuck to the back. The girl paused there, touching the pin.

"I miss school, too," the girl said. "I miss my friends."

"I've told you a million times!" the Blue Queen said. "Don't have friends! Have underlings! Friends," she said, "friends only disappoint."

This sounded like very bad advice to Fern. But the girl seemed to accept it as fact. "I know," she said, quietly. "I know."

"Good. Now where's my fur? I can't leave it here or the help will steal it."

The girl stood. "In the wardrobe," she said.

Through a crack in the doors of the wardrobe, Fern could see the trim of a fur. It began to shake and bounce. It pushed its way off the hanger and landed on the floor on its paws. Fern could see a few pairs of eyes, raccoon eyes. It scrambled to the Blue Queen, out of sight, but Fern could imagine the coat of animals clambering up her legs and arms, resting themselves on her shoulders.

The door opened, and the Blue Queen's voice called down the hall. "You two! Yes, you! With the feather dusters! I'm Fattler's special guest speaker, Ubuleen Heet!"

Fern froze. Ubuleen Heet? So that's what she meant by hiding in plain sight! The Blue Queen was in disguise as the motivational speaker! Her invitation had been sent by the Blue Queen! The Blue Queen was the head of the Secret Society of Somebodies.

"Oh, Miss Heet! What can we do for you?" a voice shouted down the hall.

"Come in here and tidy this, will you? It stinks of smoke and the awful odor of livestock, like an old barn! I have a speaking engagement, as you may know, and I can't tolerate a room like this!"

"Yes, ma'am!" they said. "We'll get to it! Right away!"

Fern tried to work out the names in her head:

THE BLUE QUEEN

UBULEEN HEET

There was only a single letter missing. "Q." Her middle initial?

So Ubuleen Heet was famous. She was the speaker! How could this be? Didn't anyone know that she was evil? That she was the Blue Queen returned, the one responsible for the dead books? That she was using the anniversary of her defeat as a soft spot in time so that she could return? Fern kept her book-hands pinned under her body, too afraid to budge.

The girl was still in the room. In fact, she was just feet away from Howard and Fern. She stood at the box, putting some of the books back into it. There was the unmistakable scent of rot, something soured or, worse, dead. She was talking to herself, repeating, "It will all be worth it in the end. It will all be worth it."

Her mother called once more, "Don't forget your red hat, Lucess, dear."

Lucess? Brine? Fern's stomach looped as if she were still on the glass elevator. She grabbed Howard's arm. He was already rigid with fear. He looked at Fern, his eyes watery. Her mind couldn't help but line up letters again.

LUCESS BRINE

BLUE

She came up with that quickly. What letters were left? "C-E-S-S R-I-N" . . . She flipped them. RINCESS. Again, she was only missing one letter.

"And, please," the Blue Queen shouted. "Don't forget to feed your father!"

Lucess walked to the fishbowl. Fern and Howard listened to her unscrew a cap and tap it on the side of the bowl.

"Here you go, Daddy," she said, and then she added in a whisper, "Soon you'll be with us. It will all be worth it!"

Then she walked to the other side of the bed and started rummaging through her suitcase, for her red hat, no doubt. The red hat tumbled to the floor just beside Howard's head. When she bent down to retrieve it, Howard gave a small gasp.

Lucess whipped up the dust ruffle. Her sharp face appeared beneath the bed. She stared at Howard and Fern, dazed. Fern was ready to scream if necessary. She was already stiffening for Lucess's attack.

But Lucess's face went soft. "You're here," she said.

"You?" Fern said. "It was *you* trying to shut the books? Your mother is—"

"Ubuleen Heet," Lucess said.

"The Blue Queen?"

She nodded.

"Middle initial 'Q'?" Fern asked.

She nodded again.

"And yours starts with, let me guess, the letter 'P'?"

"My middle name is Princess," she said. "I was the one who planted the invitation, and I was supposed to make you want to be a Somebody, and I was supposed to find out your weaknesses and report them."

"And what did you report?" Fern asked.

"I reported that you didn't have any real weaknesses. I kind of admired you back in Mrs. Fluggery's class," she said.

"Really?" Fern said.

Lucess whispered, "Don't come to the secret society meeting."

"I don't know where it is, even," Fern said.

"The news will find you, but ignore it. Listen, whatever you do, don't come."

"Lucess?" the Blue Queen's voice thundered down the hallway.

And then the dust ruffle dropped back into place and she disappeared.

"I've got it! Coming!" Lucess called to her mother. Her shoes clicked across the now-slate floor and out the door.

PONY ON THE LOOSE

FERN AND HOWARD STARED AT THEIR HANDS. The pages had disappeared and shrunk back into fingers, but faint ridges still existed where the bindings had been.

Howard was tight-lipped with concentration. "What just happened?"

"I think she almost got our souls," Fern said, still dazed. She opened and closed her hands to make sure they still worked.

"Lucess Brine is here! How did you know her initials?"

"I was working some things out in my head. That's all. The letters almost added up." Fern said, "Her mother is the Blue Queen. She's awful, Howard. She could take over the Anybodies again. She ruled once for eleven days, and that's when they thought that she killed Merton Gretel, but he isn't dead. He's the fish in the bowl on the nightstand—or, well, almost all of him is the fish in the bowl on the nightstand. A good bit of his soul is gone."

"We've got to get out of here," Howard said, patting the pony. "And you can't go to that meeting!"

There wasn't time for further discussion. The door banged open, and the room filled with the sound of a badly squeaking wheel, and, above it, a woman speaking. "Well, wait till I tell my Artie that I talked to Ubuleen Heet!"

Fern peeked out to see two women wearing gray dresses with white stockings and aprons, pushing a cart of supplies with a hanging bag full of laundry. The woman with the high-pitched snippy voice was small and tough-looking, like a little wrestler (if wrestlers wore gray dresses with white stockings and aprons). The other woman was heavyset and looked like she'd been shoved into her dress with excessive force—a kind of excessive force that had dislodged most of her bun. It looked like she had suffered a mighty explosion on the back of her head.

Fern wondered if they would notice the little jars on

the desk—the jars filled with the compressed souls, those little glowing eggs. The Blue Queen had left out a row of five jars, all filled to the brim. Fern wanted to rescue those souls. And she wanted to save Merton, too. But how?

The exploded-bun woman said, "And she's right about the smell of this place! How awful! Worse than the flying monkeys' rooms!"

At the mention of flying monkeys, Howard grabbed Fern's arm and squeezed with full-panic force. Fern wasn't afraid of flying monkeys. I mean, perhaps she would have been, but now she could only think of the Blue Queen's voice, the awful laughter, the way she said the word "souls," and the souls themselves being tugged from their pages.

"Well, I told Fattler I didn't want to clean up after them flying monkeys anymore, but he says that them flying monkeys make good bellhops. 'Can't ask for better speed.' And I gave a huff and then, you know what he says next?"

"What?" the exploded-bun woman asked.

"He says that them flying monkeys are the least of his problems." The wrestler woman added in a whisper, "You notice how the stairs in the lobby were all sopping wet. I heard it's 'cause the stairway transformed into a waterfall."

"Do you think Fattler made a mistake?"

"Well, some are saying he's just lost his touch. But do you know what else I heard? Someone told me he said he never was a genius, that it was all a big mix-up and he's just ordinary."

Fern shut her eyes tight. Fattler. He couldn't be ordinary! She'd read all about how he was a legend in a long line of legends, famous for grand Anybody hospitality and innovations. He didn't need to rely on anyone but himself. What would he think of what had just happened in this room, in his very own hotel? He needed to know that Ubuleen Heet was the Blue Queen, was killing books, was probably bound to ruin his hotel, and worse. Fern had to get to Fattler before the Queen did.

The exploded-bun woman said, "I heard some computers turned into tortoises and waddled into the swimming pool."

"Yes, yes, a whole school of tortoises, and when Fattler tried to transform them back, they short-circuited." The wrestler woman went on, "But Fattler's keeping a lid on it. He doesn't want people to know."

Was Fattler really in trouble? Fern thought back to her grandmother's warning: *Fern will be a target.* A target for what? Fern wondered now.

The two women pulled out aerosol cans and started spraying the air. One revved the vacuum, and that made the pony stir and then wake up. He tottered to a stand, then shook his mane. He started to bolt out from under the bed.

Fern grabbed him and said, "No, come back," just at the same moment that the vacuum cleaner plug popped from the wall. The vacuum died, and Fern's voice rang across the room.

"What was that noise?" the exploded-bun woman said.

Fern clamped her hands over her mouth, which meant that the pony was free. He bounded out from under the bed. The wrestler screamed like she'd seen a mouse. Fern watched the pony dodge the exploded-bun woman's broom and slip out the door to run loose in the hotel.

"It come from under the bed," the wrestler screamed.

The exploded-bun woman marched to Howard's side of the bed with her broom in hand. She took the stick end and was about to drive it into Howard's belly when Fern grabbed his arm and pulled him. Howard clutched the book and they both rolled out the other side. Howard scrambled back over the bed, the wrestler woman reaching for him.

"Vermin! Stowaways!" she screamed. "Get 'em!"

While the wrestler woman screamed and the exploded-bun woman swung her broom around like a bat at

Howard, Fern dashed to the desk. She grabbed two jars and shoved them quickly into her sweatshirt pockets. Howard swayed this way and that, until he got a straight shot out of the room. Fern turned to go grab the fishbowl, but there was no time. She jumped onto the cart, rolled across the room, then hopped off. Fern and Howard both ran as fast as they could down the blue then pink then orangey hall.

PART 3

THE IVORY KEY

OH, CONVENTIONS!

SOMETIMES I FORGET THAT YOU'RE STILL YOUNG.
This is because you are such a wise and thoughtful
reader. But the fact is, that despite your maturity, you
are not a grown-up and you probably do not sell flood
insurance or condos in Florida. You probably do not
dress up in itchy wool pants, carry a musket and do
Civil War reenactments. And you probably do not
belong to the High Order of Hairless Persian Cat
Breeders. And because you are not shouldering the
burdens of grown-up life (as if kid life doesn't have its
own burdens! Ha!), you have probably never been to a
convention.

Conventions can be big, sprawling, ugly ordeals that

take place mainly in hotels. Much like any good birth-day party, a convention always has a theme, but unlike a good birthday party, it often has little joy (and rarely cake with cursive lettering and candles). Amid meetings and booths (of freebie pencils with slogans printed on them in tiny letters), there's often a motivational speaker, who sometimes gets so lathered up about the theme (which might be floods, or condos in Boca, or muskets, or hairless cats) that he or she spits when speaking loudly into a microphone.

Ubuleen Heet was this year's speaker at the Anybodies convention.

Fern and Howard ran down flight after flight of stairs. When they got to the bottom, Fern said, "Hand me the book." She held on to its heavy binding and concen-trated. There in the empty stairwell, *The Art of Being Anybody* shrank and hardened and reddened until it was the size and shape of an apple. Fern shoved it into one of her sweatshirt pockets, which bulged because it now held not only a jar of souls but an apple, too.

"We can't have *The Art of Being Anybody* paraded around in this crowd," she said.

"Good thinking. And it was heavy, too. My arms are tired."

They took a deep breath and opened the door at the bottom of the stairs to find themselves in a wide corridor, right in front of a life-sized picture of Ubuleen Heet. They both jumped back, and then realized she was only life*like*—not real. It was simply announcing the time of her speech in the amphitheater later that evening.

To get to the lobby, Fern and Howard had to pass down the wide corridor. It was filled with booths manned by people in smart suits. Fern and Howard had stopped running. Instead they strode along in a purposefully rushed way. Fern knew that if you look purposefully rushed, you don't have time to answer questions like, *Do your parents know you're walking around loose like this? Do you kids even have a room in this hotel? Could you please show me your key?*

Still breathless from their escape, they took this time to whisper to each other.

Howard asked, "Do books have souls? Was she dragging the souls out of books and and. . . ?"

"Leaving the books for dead?"

"Do you think?"

Fern nodded.

"Why?" Howard whispered. "Why would someone do that?"

"They're her power source, I think. Dorathea said the Blue Queen needed a power source because she'd been stripped of her powers after the eleven-day rule."

"Do you think she could take over again?" Howard

asked nervously. "She makes me feel like I'm going to throw up. She's worse than that elevator ride."

"I don't know," Fern said. "We've got to find Fattler and warn him. She can't get that key—whatever it is."

"How will we find Fattler and tell him what's going on? I mean, we aren't even supposed to be here, Fern," Howard said.

"We still have to warn him somehow," Fern said.

"Let's just disappear. Slink off. Hide out. It's safer."

"Do you want to head to Gravers? The Drudgers have court orders, you know."

"You're right," Howard said.

Fern zipped up, put on her hood and pulled the strings. "And keep an eye out for Dorathea and the Bone. They'll be looking for us everywhere, I'm sure."

Howard hunched up his shoulders and looked around. "Court orders," he muttered. "Court orders."

They shuffled quickly through the brisk crowd. It seemed like a good spot to be, lost in all the people. They listened to bits of conversation:

"Target market," she heard.

And, "Tom Hanks was at the bagel table."

"In full animation?" someone else asked.

Fern wanted to see Tom Hanks, fully animated or not. She didn't hear the answer. The people bustled by.

Another group was talking about the motivational

speaker: "She's going to teach us to embrace our inner something. I can't remember. But isn't that wonderful?"

"I don't want her telling me to embrace anything," Howard said. His eyes darted all over the lobby, taking everything in.

"You like it here, don't you?" Fern asked.

"Of course not," Howard said.

A woman idling by a booth offering Peace and Tranquility—"a soap that works right into your skin, transforming you to a place of pure calm"—caught Fern's eye and gave a wink. And because it's a natural instinct for an Anybody to wink back at an Anybody who's winked at them, Fern felt her eye snap shut for a split second. The woman was wearing a smoking jacket, with fancy overlapped letters stitched onto its chest pocket. Fern didn't like the woman, and she stuck closer to Howard because of her.

One young woman was selling Anybody Water supplies. "You just buy the bottle, fill it with tap water, and it will instantly transform into fresh mountain spring water from the Alps." There were bankers claiming they could transform stock portfolios. Marriage counselors, beauty consultants, body coaches, dentists—all with transforming products.

Most people were gathered around one booth. Howard pulled Fern toward the crowd.

"What do you think they're selling?" he said.

The salesman seemed like he had no need of any of the other booths, or like he'd already benefited from what they had to offer. He looked smiley, fit, beautiful, in love, rich and well hydrated. He said, "This is revolutionary! It's proven to be completely effective! The Correct-O-Cure spray. When sprayed liberally on a person or object that has been transformed, it destabilizes and returns the person or object to its original state, fixing any wrongs incurred during the period of change. In other words, transformations are reversed!"

"That can't be right," Fern said.

"Yes it can," Howard said. "That's the best thing I've ever heard of. It gives you a break, at least, from all that crazy Anybody behavior! A break! That's the product for me!" Howard waddled through the crowd and got two small sample spray bottles.

"It's probably a scam. It can't work!" Fern said, keeping an eye on the salesman.

"You never know." Howard shoved the minibottles into his pocket.

The salesman winked at Fern with a crooked smile. Fern winked back, of course. She had no choice. She noticed that the salesman had the same looping letters stitched onto his blazer. Fern stared at them more closely while he went on with his spiel, all sugary, do-good and fake. Fern stared until the letters became distinct from one another: SSS.

"The Secret Society of Somebodies," Fern whispered, backing away.

"What?" Howard said.

"C'mon," Fern said. "Let's keep going."

They pushed their way through the crowd and found themselves on a golden-railed landing with two sets of turning staircases on either side.

"The lobby," she said. "The grand lobby of Willy Fattler's Underground Hotel."

WILLY FATTLER'S GRAND LOBBY—
FLYING MONKEYS AND ALL!

WHEN HOWARD AND FERN HAD REACHED THE middle of the bustling lobby, they stopped and let it all swirl around them: the massive glittering chandelier; the small orchestra in one corner playing something antique and lilting; the fountain bubbling in the middle of the floor; plush golden overstuffed chairs beneath huge paintings of men and women in white wigs, holding pug-faced doggies; a row of revolving doors in constant twirl at the front; a fleet of elevators *bing*ing wildly on one wall; a bank of fast-talking clerks—they were wearing powdered wigs too, as were the flying monkeys. (The wrestler woman had been telling the truth about them after all.) The monkeys scooped up suitcases in their clawed feet and flapped overhead and up the large spiral staircases.

Some very elegant Anybodies sipped wine by the fountain, picking at the food display—chocolate-shellacked fruit, plus candies and grapes and cheeses. Other Anybodies, tourists, clutched cameras and gaped. A few were whispering and pointing at a man with dark hair, shuffling through the lobby with some children in tow. One of the kids was complaining about an itchy tag, and so the man stopped. He pulled the kid's tag out of his shirt. His hands suddenly turned into a complicated instrument filled with sharp pointy knives and scissory things. He quickly snipped the child's shirt tag. His hand went back to normal. A tourist waved to him excitedly, and a purple top hat appeared on the man's head. He tipped it. The purple hat disappeared, and he scurried out of the lobby with his kids.

"That was Johnny Depp," Fern whispered to Howard.

"Johnny who?"

"The famous actor!"

"Don't know him!"

Fern didn't take the time to explain. There was too much to see. Fern was drawn to the huge map on the wall opposite the food display. The map was multilayered:

New York City above, and the city beneath the city below. Fern spotted the castle right off. It was located beneath an open field at Central Park. She touched the spire and the spot in Central Park where, at this very moment, Fern thought, a family might have just spread out a blanket for a picnic.

"I'm hungry," Howard said, pulling Fern toward the heaps of delicacies. "Look at it all!"

Fern hadn't realized how hungry she was. She and Howard stood there for a moment, just taking in the beautiful colors, the scents—everything polished in either sugar or chocolate or a colored glaze. Even the ham was chocolate frosted.

Fern looked closely, taking a deep breath.

Howard grabbed a plate and started filling it. "One for you, two for me." He was scooping as many chocolate-covered things as possible from the enormous mountain of goodies.

Just as Fern was about to take a bite, a couple leaned in close to her. "Oh, hello! So great to see you here," the woman whispered.

"Yes, looking forward to your joining," the man said.

They were a well-groomed couple who smelled particularly sweet and fruity. They had tidy haircuts and broad smiles.

"You know not to go to the speech, don't you?" the

woman said. "It's for the others. The lesser masses."

"The lesser masses?"

The woman flitted her hand in the air. "You know, those who are clearly *not* Somebodies. Let them be hypnotized to think less of themselves! Not us. We're ready to go up! Aren't we?" The woman nodded her tidy haircut at Howard, who was standing nearby, trying to pretend he wasn't paying attention. Fern now saw both the Triple S logos on their blazers.

"Up?" Fern asked.

"Yes, yes! Straight up!" She pointed to the ceiling.

"Congratulations on your selection into the society!" the man said, his smile aglow. "Ubuleen is pleased, I'm sure of it! You'll be a Somebody soon. Like us!"

A Somebody? She thought back to Lucess Brine in Mrs. Fluggery's class, and how she used to call her a nobody, saying, *Don't you wish you were a somebody?* Fern *had* wanted to be a somebody—how happy she'd been about the invitation! But now, she *didn't* want to be a somebody—not like these Somebodies. What was the Triple S exactly, and did they really know Ubuleen Heet? Did they know she was the Blue Queen? And what could they possibly mean by *We're ready to go up?* Fern wanted to tell the couple that they might *think* they were friends with Ubuleen Heet, but she didn't have friends. She didn't believe in it. Or were they just as evil as she was? Fern decided not to ask any questions, though. She didn't want to align herself with the Triple S and Ubuleen Heet. "I don't know what you're talking about," she said, trying to sound polite.

The couple nodded. "That's right," the woman said. "Of course not!"

"Hush, hush," said the man, laughing as if Fern had told a joke, and they waltzed off into a group of Somebodies in Triple S blazers.

"Do you know them?" Howard asked.

"The Secret Society," Fern muttered, as one of the women at the front desk nodded at her knowingly, the "S's" on her blazer shrunken to a small emblem that was hardly visible. "They're after me."

Just then the chandelier overhead flickered. All the chattering Anybodies hushed, overly ripe with joy. Two more women with Triple S blazers raised their fingers to their lips and shushed right at Fern, wearing their smiles. Even the orchestra fell silent—was the clarinetist wearing a Triple S blazer? Fern felt panicked. Was she just imagining that Somebodies were everywhere now?

The silver fork in Howard's hand disappeared, and the mountain of goodies shrank into a row of blue plates. On each plate was a small dollop of some orange meat with a zigzag of white sauce on top.

"Oooh! Ahhh!" the Anybodies sighed joyfully.

"What happened?" Fern asked.

"The food shrank!" Howard said, staring at his plate.

"Oh, how very modern!" a woman next to them shrieked.

Fern and Howard looked around the lobby. Fern didn't have time to look for Triple S blazers for the moment, because everything was changing, twisting, churning, paling and brightening, too. The change was sweeping in waves from one side of the room to the other. The food and lighting went in the first wave. The chandelier became a sculpture of fluorescent tubing.

"This is what I've read about!" Fern said. "This is Fattler's genius—an ever-changing hotel! Isn't it . . . amazing!"

Across the room a man shouted. A woman screamed and pointed. Fern looked at the spot of the commotion. She saw the miniature pony in full-speed gallop, hurtling in their direction.

"Look!" Fern said. "He's back!"

Because of the pony, Fern and Howard weren't prepared for the wave that followed—the flooring, from marble to metallic tiles. The Anybodies all seemed to know to step over the new flooring as it washed past. Even the pony leaped at the right moment. Fern was trying to reach for the pony, though, and Howard was

trying to balance his food. They were pitched up into the air by the new flooring. They fell hard. Fern and Howard exchanged a look of pure astonishment. They both glanced over their shoulders, but the pony was gone. Fern patted her pockets. The apples and the jars of egg-souls were safe. The next wave was coming. They could feel it in the air. They scrambled quickly to their feet.

This wave turned the paintings of people in wigs holding pugs into rows of white canvases, each entitled *Pink Canvas*. The orchestra was replaced by a performance artist—a woman cutting the hair off a Barbie doll. The flying monkeys no longer had white wigs. They had spiked Mohawks. A final wave whittled the overstuffed chairs into sleek cushioned planks, and the fountain disappeared completely. In its place was a spotlight on nothing.

Fern was stunned. "It's all changed!" she said. "Transformed!"

"Into what?" Howard said, looking down at the squares of orange meat. "Can they change it back?"

Howard popped a bunch of the orange meat squares into his mouth, even though it was clearly the kind of thing you weren't supposed to eat in bulk. "Not bad," he said. "I mean, it's not chocolate-covered ham, but it's not bad."

"Pretty good, I'd say." It was a man wearing a pair of bifocals, and a Triple S blazer. "Hello there, Fern," he whispered, and then sauntered off.

"Do you know him?" Howard asked.

Fern shook her head.

As the commotion from the lobby's transformation settled, there was a new commotion on the second floor, where the two winding staircases met in the middle. Everyone was suddenly twisting to get a look.

"Good day!" The voice boomed like it was being blasted out of department store speakers throughout the lobby. But actually, it came from one spot, a large mouth—big as the kind you'd find on a grouper, which is a kind of fish. The mouth was located just below a waxy blond moustache and a bobble of a nose—a nose that on this large flushed face seemed more decorative than something you'd actually use for breathing. The man was rosy and jolly and jowly and robust. He was all these things at once; he was a perfect example of a rosejollyjowlybust. Or almost. There was something skittish in his eyes, a watery, nearly teary nervousness. But he still spoke with great force. "So wonderful to see you all here today at Willy Fattler's Underground Hotel!"

Fern knew, straightaway, that he was Willy Fattler. She'd seen pictures of him in *The Art of Being Anybody*, Chapter 16. There were photos of him and his father, also named Willy Fattler, and his grandfather, also named Willy Fattler, and his great-grandfather, also named, you guessed it, Willy Fattler. He was just as Fern had pictured him: big and bellowing, in the center of it all.

"Welcome to the grand extravaganza! Where you will find that you *can* please everyone, *if* you offer enough choices!" He turned then with a majestic flourish. "May I introduce Ubuleen Heet. The hottest new motivational speaker! She will, no doubt, change our lives!"

Ubuleen strode forward and waved. Fern could see Lucess standing behind her. Ubuleen was stroking the fur of her coat, which was not live raccoons now at all, just a fur coat.

"Please come and hear her speak later today in the amphitheater, the largest Anybodies amphitheater known to Anybodies worldwide, where guests buy tickets to the grand imagination! Enjoy your stay at Willy Fattler's Underground Hotel," he bellowed. And then he added in an urgent whisper, as if he couldn't stop himself even though he wanted to, "Now offering day spa specials at a special rate, perfect for a weekend getaway."

What did that have to do with anything? Fern had to talk to him, but he was surrounded by Anybodies in Triple S blazers. Even as she tried to push her way through the crowd, Fattler backed away from the railing, took Ubuleen by the arm, and they disappeared through a pair of tall mirrored doors. Just then the fluorescent tubing overhead flickered into a sagging, rusty lamp. The food swelled into pots of all things meaty and beany.

"We've got to follow Fattler," Fern said.

Fern turned to Howard. "Watch out for the—" Fern grabbed Howard's arm, and they jumped together as the metallic tiles flapped and changed into worn wood.

The woman giving Barbie doll haircuts morphed into a player piano with a loud, warped, tinkling sound. The paintings repainted themselves into portraits of horses and stern-faced outlaws. The folks at the check-in counter became surly. The women clerks wore old-fashioned dresses and the men ten-gallon hats. They slapped down old keys, telling guests that they weren't allowed to shoot on the premises. Two of the flying monkeys, dressed in dusty vests and worn denim, started a brawl, and the concierge had to break it up. The concierge threw out a rabble-rousing monkey through the saloon doors that had replaced the revolving doors.

Fattler was escorting Ubuleen and Lucess from the lobby. A man in saggy pants, wearing a holster with pistols in it, was breaking up the crowd for them. "Walk this way, Ubuleen, Lucess!"

The people around Fern were whispering about Ubuleen. "It's her!"

Howard looked down at what he was holding: a tin cup of something beany. "I don't really like beans," he said.

Howard pulled out one of his bottles of Correct-O-Cure and sprayed the cupful of beans. The spray stunk like burnt plastic.

"What are you doing?" Fern asked. "We need to get to Fattler!"

"Trying to get these beans to turn back into chocolate. That's what, of course!"

"It's a scam," Fern said. "Let's go!"

"Don't be like that, Fern." He shook the bottle again and sprayed, coughing because of the burnt plastic stink. The beans stayed beans.

Fern shrugged. "Give up," she said.

Howard sighed heavily, shoving the half-empty bottle back into his pocket with the other minibottle. "You know, everyone has to have faith in something!"

"Let's go," she said, rushing past a few beaming Somebodies. "We've got to keep Fattler in sight! We have to warn him!" Howard wasn't budging. Fern grabbed his arm. "Come on," she said, but he was frozen to the spot.

Howard had made his own discovery. His face had gone slack. He could barely speak. He tugged on Fern's sleeve. "Dorathea," he said, "and the Bone!" Howard pointed to the other side of the lobby. The Bone had flyers in his hands. Fern could see that the flyers had Howard's and Fern's pictures on them—their awful school pictures. *Does everyone have to use those?* Fern thought.

She and Howard ducked behind a clump of tourists. Two police officers stood near Dorathea and the Bone. They, too, had flyers in their hands. Dorathea and the Bone, looking shaky and lost themselves, talked to the officers for a moment, and then, refusing the help of a flying monkey, they carried their old lumpy suitcases into the crowd, straight toward where Howard and Fern were hiding.

"We've been found out!" Howard said. "They'll take us back! We'll end up in military academy! Court orders!"

Fern grabbed Howard and pulled him quickly into the thick of the crowd that was shuffling through the lobby, which was changing yet again. They cruised around very low tables of steaming tea and a Kabuki dancer heading away from the front desk, where the female attendants were now wearing shiny kimonos and stiff arrangements of black hair. The two pushed to the other side, but not without getting tangled up. Fern fell in such a way that the jars in her pockets went crashing to the floor. The jars broke and the little eggs rolled in all different directions. The apple, too, spun off across the floor.

The crowd was so thick that people kept on marching. Clumps of Somebodies were everywhere she looked. Fern had no time to pick up all the egglike souls and the shards of glass. She grabbed the apple just as the crowd was dragging her and Howard along in a strong current. Dorathea and the Bone were closing in. Fern jumped up, grabbing Howard's arm on the way. They ran forward and found themselves shoved into a revolving door that kicked them out onto the sidewalk, into the city beneath the city itself.

3

A TRANSFORMATION

FROM THE GLASS ELEVATOR, THE CITY BENEATH the city had looked like it was made of the things that a city is normally made of: cement, tar, stone, brick, scaffolding, movie-poster paste, and a fine coating of unidentifiable grit. But when Fern and Howard actually made their way along the sidewalks, they noticed that the materials of the city beneath the city were softer, stretchier, squishier. For example, when Fern and Howard saw the giant billboard with their pictures on it and the word MISSING printed over their heads, and they dipped into an alley and leaned against the building's brickish wall, the wall wasn't stiff. In fact, it mushed around them. The city had the squishiness of a fat bottom in spandex.

Did Fern and Howard have a lot of time to contemplate

the fat-bottom-in-spandex character of the city, or its sky of dirt that sometimes crumbled a bit in one area or another, causing people to pop open umbrellas? No, they did not. The flyers were posted on telephone poles, on the sides of cabs. Teenagers on corners were passing them out to people on the street who'd glance, and sometimes shake their heads—*Poor dears!*—before shoving the flyers in their pockets.

"Where are we going to go?" Howard asked.

"I don't know," Fern said, but then she realized that she kind of did. She'd pretty much memorized the fold-out map in *The Art of Being Anybody*. She thought of all the places she'd seen in the map: Melvin's Laundromat and Dry Cleaner's, China Star Restaurant, Bing Chubb's Ballpark, Hyun's Dollar Fiesta, Jubber's Pork Rind Juke Joint, and Blessed Holy Trinity Catholic Church and Bingo Hall. Could they hide in any of those spots and not be recognized?

"We'll be spotted. We need to transform if we're going to be able to get close to Fattler. We can only go around if we're in disguise." (Now, this is something I understand completely, dressed as I am at this very moment as a failed investment banker.)

"Oh, no!" Howard said. "I'm no good at transformations! I can't do it!"

"I don't know if I can either. I've only done it once before."

158

"But it was a good one," Howard said. "I mean, a grizzly bear!"

"I'm going to try to transform," Fern said. "I'm going to give it a whirl. And . . ." She looked up and saw a large trash bin. Sitting next to it was a beaten newspaper. "You'll just have to hide behind the newspaper until we can find a real disguise for you."

She ran to the newspaper, grabbed it and gave it to Howard.

"Okay," Howard said.

Fern tried to remember how she'd felt the first time she'd transformed something. Every Anybody knew that the world was in constant flux, always changing. Fern had to concentrate on that. She had to capture that feeling within her. It seemed easier having been in Willy Fattler's Underground Hotel, where everything was always changing shape. Fern loved it, but it made her feel a bit lost, too. If everything was changing all the time, was there anything she could truly count on? She needed something loyal.

It was that moment, when her mind hit on the word "loyal," that Fern felt her teeth lengthen and her tongue grow longer and thinner. Her body went squat. Her legs and arms shrunk. She looked down at her feet—paws, furry paws. All her clothes had turned into fur. The apple—a disguise for *The Art of Being Anybody*—plopped on the ground and rolled to a stop.

She was a short, brown mutt. She looked up at Howard.

He smiled and patted her head. "I always wanted a dog," he said, grabbing the apple.

Fern barked, meaning, *I'm not your pet, Howard! I'm still Fern! And I have a plan.* She trotted down the alley.

"Where are you going, doggie? Cute little doggie!"

Fern turned around and growled.

"Okay, okay!" Howard said. "I'm coming!"

At the end of the alley, she stopped, turned, and pawed at Howard's trousers. He picked her up and used the beaten newspaper to cover his face.

"Where to?" he asked.

Fern wasn't sure. She barked, meaning, *Just hurry! Something will come to me.* Fern sat as upright as possible in his arms. When they came to an intersection, Howard started to go straight. Fern growled. He turned left. She gave a happy bark. Howard blew past a young man handing out MISSING flyers and then past a group of tourist Somebodies posing for a picture.

They rushed up one street and down another, trying to dodge the people handing out flyers. Strangely enough, Fern was enjoying herself. She loved the bustle of the city beneath the city. She loved zipping past the places she'd only imagined. She loved the way the city seemed to be creating itself just for her, corner after surprising new corner. She lost track of time. How long

160

had they been winding down the streets?

Howard wasn't enjoying himself. He kept saying things like "Where are we going?" "I'm exhausted." "You're heavier than I thought you'd be." "This isn't helping! We need a low-risk option. A plan!"

Why couldn't Howard just have fun? Dogs had fun. Howard was sometimes very Drudgerly. She thought of Howard as a future accountant, how he always knew exactly how much money he had in his wallet at all times. His wallet! Fern had forgotten about that. She didn't have any money, but Howard did. They could *buy* a disguise. Fern knew just the spot.

Fern yipped.

"What is it?" Howard asked. "Do you have a plan finally?"

She yipped again, and directed him with more yipping.

Hyun's Dollar Fiesta was a ways off, but Howard had more zip now that he knew he had a destination. Finally they found themselves in front of the window. It was filled with everything you could imagine: plungers, marbles, hairnets, plastic toy chipmunks, colored nylons, zippers, compasses, small moose statues, tins of chopped liver, tins of rubber cement, tins of cotton balls, tins of tin, and banana-scented candles.

"Here?" Howard asked.

She nodded.

In they went.

HYUN'S DOLLAR FIESTA

HOWARD CARRIED FERN, ALL PRICKED EARS AND pink panting tongue, to the back of the store. They passed a sign posted on the door that read NO DOGS ALLOWED, just under yet another one of those MISSING flyers. Howard didn't like to break rules. It made him uncomfortable. The place was crowded, however, and no one seemed to notice the boy carrying the dog. Also, it should be noted, there's a singleness of focus at bargain stores that cannot be fully explained by scientists. But it's been theorized that if Americans could shift their singleness of focus from dollar items at bargain stores to the energy crisis, it would be solved by now. (I'm guilty of this myself. I have to remind myself to breathe in those places.)

Fern felt her tail wagging behind her. It was a strange feeling, this thing swinging around. She pointed her wet dog nose at a pair of sunglasses on a spinning rack. Howard said "excuse me" to a few shoppers and tried them on. They looked good enough.

She pointed her nose at a winter cap. Howard said "excuse me" to some kids, picked it up from a pile and put it on his head. All good.

She pointed her nose at a fake ponytail.

"No," Howard said. "That's where I draw the line!"

Fern growled.

"Shhh!" Howard said. "We'll be found out!"

She growled again, a little louder.

Howard said excuse me to a teenager, grabbed the fake ponytail and clipped it to the hair at the nape of his neck. "Okay?" he muttered angrily. "Happy now?"

Then there was a voice right behind him. "You talk dog?" the voice said in a heavy Korean accent.

Howard and Fern turned around to see Hyun himself. He was ancient, probably over a hundred years old. He was thin, and in response to the decision that faces all elderly men (Should I wear my pants above my stomach or below?) he went with above—just below his armpits—using a tightly cinched belt to keep the pants from dropping. He had white hair and intense eyes. He wore a Hyun's Dollar Fiesta T-shirt with a pin on his chest that read HELLO MY NAME IS HYUN.

163

"Um," Howard said. "No, I don't talk dog. Not fluently."

Hyun shook his head, as if this wasn't really what he'd meant. "No dogs in Hyun's Dolla' Fiesta. It Hyun rule."

"Sorry," Howard said.

"You pay all that at cash register." Hyun said each word with emphasis.

"I will. I'm on my way there now," Howard said, passing by.

Someone interrupted. "Where are your stuffed reptiles?"

"Stuff reptile! Aisle four!" Hyun shouted, and Howard thought that was the end of it. He headed for the cashier.

"Wait!" Hyun said.

Howard stopped and turned slowly, wincing behind his sunglasses.

"I know dog," Hyun said.

"You know how to speak dog?" Howard asked.

"No!" Hyun said. He walked toward Howard, his bad knee buckling.

Someone interrupted. "Where are your singing erasers?"

"Singing eraser! Aisle three!" Hyun shouted. Then he whispered to Howard, "I know dog. This dog. This Fern dog."

Howard glanced around.

"Follow me," Hyun said. Howard followed anxiously. Fern started to shake. Was Hyun going to turn them in? He seemed like the type, frankly, with his Hyun rule and his tight belt. He walked back to the door at the end of aisle two amid a barrage of questions:

"Where are your hermit crab condos?"

"Hermit crab condo! Aisle nine!"

"Where are your poodle hammocks?"

"Poodle hammock! With hermit crab condo!"

"Where are your nitroglycerin tablets?"

Nitroglycerin tablets! Mrs. Fluggery? Fern's and Howard's heads whipped around. No, no, it was another old lady with large hair and a penchant for nitroglycerin tablets. It was just a coincidence. (Sometimes there are coincidences in life!)

"Nitroglycerin tablet! Aisle seven!"

Hyun's office in the back of the store was tiny, so tiny that he could have sold offices that size on aisle three. Hyun sat down in his very small chair pulled up to his very small desk. "You disgrace to Anybodies," Hyun said to Howard. "You shame Anybodies." He shook his head slowly, the skin at his neck wagging. "Sunglasses. Hat. Fake hair." Fern had to admit that Hyun was right. Howard was Howard.

"Are you going to turn us in?" Howard asked.

165

"Turn you in? Ha! No. You two important to history. I just help history along. I play my part." He stared at Howard. "I don't want turn you in. I want turn you into something else!"

Fern barked. She wanted to know how Hyun knew that they were part of history. Did he know about the Blue Queen? Did he know that she was going to do battle?

He smiled at her. "I know much. I know history. I so old I am history!" (This is one of the advantages that old people have. It's what makes them sly when you don't expect it!) "You need have respect for where you are—this city beneath the city! We are Anybodies, and you got to respect the art." Hyun took out a big watch on a long chain. He told Howard to look at it while he swung it back and forth.

"What do you want to turn me into?" Howard asked.

"This will be temporary. It only last short time. To make choice, I rely on inspiration!"

Howard didn't like the idea of inspiration, Fern knew. She sat on his lap as he jiggled his knees, and she watched his eyes move back and forth. "Couldn't we just try edible fake teeth?"

Hyun tsked. "Edible fake teeth!"

"Don't make me something embarrassing!" Howard said.

166

"Okay, boy. Okay!"

Hyun's voice vibrated in his throat. He held a low note. Howard's eyes glazed over slowly, and then he became a little taller, more portly. He grew a trim moustache, and a monocle and a tweed suit with a matching cap. Suddenly he was holding a leash connected to a collar around Fern's neck.

"What am I then?" Howard said in a deep voice with a British accent.

"You from a place where they don't want to be embarrassed," Hyun said. "You are prominent member of British society. You use Fern dog for fox hunts."

"Blast it!" Howard said, standing up, fiddling with his moustache. "Am I to go about in this getup? Seriously?"

"Use it quickly. It not last long."

"I hope that's a promise!" Howard said.

Fern had the feeling they were done here. She gave a little pull on her leash. Howard said quietly, "Thank you, sir! Cheerio!" And he groaned at his own accent.

There was a knock at the door, and a voice. "Where are your glow-in-the-dark toilet seats?"

"Glow-in-dark toilet seat!" Hyun shouted through the door. "Aisle fi'!"

And then he said to Fern and Howard in a relaxed voice with no hint of a Korean accent at all: "Hey, look, I know you're hiding from the authorities, and I just want to tell you this: don't get too deep into transformation. That's the mistake all those Anybodies make. I mean, you've really got to be yourself in this life. You have to rely on something deep inside."

Fern cocked her dog head. Did he just lose his accent? Did he just say that you've got to be yourself in this life?

"But—but," Howard sputtered. "Where'd your accent go? Aren't you—"

"Korean, sure, second generation. I grew up in Hackensack. My real name's Arnold."

"But why do you talk like that out there? Why do you call yourself Hyun?" Howard asked.

"Oh, that!" He shook his head. "People like it. It makes them feel like I'm a real dream-driven, hard-working immigrant. Would you have believed how wise I am without the accent? You trusted me more because of it. Didn't you?"

Fern guessed he was right. She'd liked the accent.

"But—but," Howard said. "You're telling us to be ourselves when you're not, *and* you just helped me turn into this British fop!" Fern could tell that Howard didn't even know what a fop was. The Britishness had just kicked into overdrive.

"For example, which sounds wiser: A. Don't be an idiot. Use the brain. That's why it's there." He tapped his head. "Or B. You are temple and the brain is altar. Worship there."

It was obvious; "B" sounded much wiser. There was no reason even to answer the question.

"Trust me," Hyun-Arnold said. "Authenticity is really hard to fake. And"—he sighed—"it wears on you." The phone rang, shaking his little desk. He looked at it wearily and then, resigned to the task, picked it up. "Hyun Dollar Fiesta!" Hyun-Arnold shouted. "I help you!" He kept his eyes on Howard and Fern—the British society man and his fox-hunting dog. Then he covered the phone with one hand, and said, "Don't be an idiot. Use the brain. That's why it's there. You are temple and your mind is altar. Worship there. Okay?"

Howard and Fern both nodded.

"Go now," Hyun-Arnold said, and gave a small wave—a small, sad wave.

Howard waved back, and Fern lifted her furry paw.

THE BRAIN AS ALTAR

WHEN YOU WALK DOWN BUSY CITY STREETS wearing tweed and a monocle, holding a dog and a red apple, people tend to nod to you, quite formally. Some are doing it as a show of respect, others because they've been caught staring and want to make up for it. And others are clearly making fun of you. I know this because I've tried this disguise, just by chance. (I've tried almost every disguise known to man—lounge singer, psychic, phonograph needle installer.)

Howard didn't like all the attention, good or bad. He didn't like nodding back. But the newfound British manners in him wouldn't let him pass anyone by. "Good day!" he found himself saying, despite his best efforts at restraint. "Good day to you!" If his hands hadn't been full, he'd have tipped his tweed cap.

But he did like sauntering past two police officers talking outside of Jubber's Pork Rind Juke Joint without them taking any notice.

It was quite a walk back to Willy Fattler's, and by the time they were heading down Small Change Avenue in the direction they'd come, it was starting to get dark. The wind in her fur, Fern was thinking about what Hyun-Arnold had suggested in his own coded way: *Don't be an idiot. Use the brain. That's why it's there. You are temple and the brain is altar. Worship there.* He knew a lot, accent or no accent. And Fern was inclined to follow his advice. It also happened to be the only advice available. The problem was that they were trying to use their brains, of course! So what did he mean exactly?

Now that they'd transformed beyond recognition, they could have headed right back to the lobby easily enough, and pretended they were mingling while really they would be searching. However, when they got close, they noticed that Dorathea and the Bone were handing out MISSING flyers, and Howard seized up and looked at Fern.

"We can't!"

Fern gave a bark that meant *sure we can.* She jumped out of Howard's arms and started trotting forward.

"No," Howard shouted. "Don't!"

This noisy disturbance got Dorathea and the Bone's attention.

Fern barked again, but this time it didn't come out as a bark. It came out as words. "Why do you have to worry so much?" And that is when it struck her that she was no longer completely doglike. She was shaggy still, but her nails were the buds of her own human fingers. She was turning back into herself.

She looked back at Howard. He patted his head. His tweed hat was gone. He blinked his monocle from his eye.

They both ran as fast as they could toward the edge of the building. They heard the Bone shouting, "Fern! Howard! Is that you?"

"Wait!" they heard Dorathea call out.

Luckily the crowd was thick in front of the hotel. Dorathea and the Bone would have a hard time pushing through it.

Just as Fern and Howard turned the corner, they ran into a man in a Triple S blazer. "Where are you two going?" the Somebody asked. "Why not come with me?"

Howard darted around him in one direction, and Fern in the other. But the man grabbed Fern by her sweatshirt—which she was wearing again, all her fur completely gone. Fern pulled back. She looked up to see Howard take off down the side of the hotel.

"C'mon, Fern!"

"Let go!" Fern said. And the man did. He dropped his grip on her now stretched-out pocket. Fern stumbled, caught her footing and then ran on. "See you later!" he said happily.

"This way," Fern said. There was a row of doors: one marked STORAGE, one marked DROP-OFFS and one marked THIS WAY TO THE BRAIN.

The Brain. It caught her attention. "This one," she said, wondering if Hyun-Arnold had planted this as a clue all along. She reached out and grabbed the doorknob. It vibrated ever so slightly in her hand. She was ready for it to be locked, barred. She was prepared for more difficulties. She was used to the idea that nothing came easily, that they were in the kind of trouble that just brewed more trouble. That isn't always the case, you know. Sometimes when you're in trouble, something can, just accidentally, go your way. As was the case this time: She twisted the knob. The door made a little click and opened wide.

6

THE IVORY KEY

FERN AND HOWARD FOUND THEMSELVES BACK AS themselves—just Fern and Howard—in a dim room. The air held the dustiness of Fern's old school library, and there was a distant buzzing, the kind that had leaked from the library's overhead fluorescent lights. But the buzzing wasn't coming from fluorescent lights. The room was lit by a bare ceiling bulb. The buzz was mysterious.

"Is the apple okay?" Fern asked.

Howard pulled it out of his pocket and twisted it in the air.

"I'll take it," she said, taking it and putting it in her sweatshirt pocket.

"Why did you want to come in here?" Howard asked.

The room was filled with shelves, but instead of

books, as Fern usually expected of shelves, they held jars and boxes. Fern cruised the stacks and read the labels: GreasiO, Feinman's Fine Motor Oil, Geller's High-Q Ticker Tape, and Milton & Sons' Typewriter Ribbon.

"Hyun-Albert told us to use the brain, to worship there. Didn't you see the sign on the door? It said 'This way to the brain'."

"That's just weird!" Howard said.

"What if the hotel is a temple and it has a mind, a brain, where we should worship. What if?"

"That's just weird too," Howard said.

"I don't see any way to a brain!" Fern was tired. Her arms and legs felt weak, her head heavy. Transformations were exhausting. But she couldn't rest. Not now. "What time is it?" she asked Howard.

"Seven thirty," he said.

Fern was still cruising the shelves, trying to figure out where they were. She was drawn to a box marked FRAGILE in bright red letters. The lid wasn't sealed, and Fern picked up the flaps and peered inside. She saw at first a small blurry motion, as if something alive were inside of it. The overhead bulb was weak, which made it hard to see. As she looked closer, she saw wide eyes and the outline of a girl's face staring up at her. Her stomach seized. It was her own face inside the box. She gasped.

"What? What is it?" Howard asked.

Fern's heart pounded in her ears. She looked again,

and then she felt silly. "It's only a box filled with mirrors," she said. But now Fern was nervous. Just thinking that she could find herself inside a box in a storage room marked THIS WAY TO THE BRAIN in Willy Fattler's Underground Hotel scared her.

"You shouldn't be snooping," Howard said.

"I'm not snooping," Fern said. "I'm exploring. There's a difference, you know." But Fern was looking around much more nervously now, not touching anything.

"Stop exploring then. It only gets us in trouble."

Fern kept walking and came to three shelves entirely devoted to jars of what looked like honey, but these weren't labeled. Fern wanted to know what someone would need with grease, oil, typewriter ribbon, ticker tape, mirrors, and jar after jar of honey. "It's a strange place," Fern said.

She picked up a jar of honey and walked over to Howard. She sat next to him. Fern said, "Why is there so much honey? Let's eat some."

"That's the first plan that I've really liked in a long time," Howard said.

At that moment there was a distant outburst of applause, as if a group of people far off had heard what Howard said and thought it was brilliant. This wasn't the case, of course. The amphitheater must have been close to the storage room. They both stared toward one of the walls—the direction the applause had come from.

They stuck their fingers into the honey jar and started to lick them clean.

"The speech," Fern said. "Ubuleen Heet. She's started. I wish we could find out what she's up to."

"She's hypnotizing the lesser masses," Howard said. "Remember?"

Again there was a small round of applause. Howard said with a shaky smile, "They love me. What can I say?"

Fern looked around the room, taking it all in. Other than the shelves full of weird supplies, the room had a sad, old wooden chair with uneven legs propped near an unmarked door. There was the door they'd entered from the rear of the hotel, and another that read HOTEL LOBBY.

Since they'd stopped talking, Fern had felt a slight electric tension in the room. She got up and started pacing.

"Where are you going?" Howard asked to a smattering of applause. "Do you hear that buzzing?"

"Yes," she said. It sounded like static—constant and thrumming.

Howard sat down on the spindly lone chair. "We need *another* plan, Fern. I mean, are we going to stay here until we're too old for a military academy? Are we going to be runaways forever? I need a plan that relies on punctuality and strategy. We need to work like a well-oiled machine, Fern." Howard waited for some applause, but this time none came. He folded his arms across his chest.

With one hand on the wall, Fern followed the

vibrations. They seemed strongest in one area. And at that spot in the wall there was a small hole. Fern bent down to look through it and found a bee, crawling out of the hole, picking its way along on its frail insect legs. It opened its wings and flew toward the ceiling.

"A bee," Fern said. "How strange."

"I'm allergic to bees!" Howard froze in his chair, his eyes darting around the room. "Whatever part gets stung swells up like a blowfish!"

"I don't know where the bee went," Fern said. "I'm sure it isn't interested in you." She wondered if it had been lured by the unmarked honey jars.

Just then there were shuffling noises outside the door marked HOTEL LOBBY and two voices talking. Fern and Howard darted behind some shelves just as the door flew open. The room was suddenly bright from the lights in the lobby. Fern and Howard froze.

Willy Fattler strode in, a bulky man in a Triple S blazer at his side.

"The key is key," the Somebody was saying. "This is just a quick tour of the castle, you know. Ubuleen is a history buff. She'd like to see all that the city has to offer. And you're the man with connections." Now Fern knew what the key was to—the castle. Her castle. She shook her head. *Don't give him the key*, she thought. *Don't give him the key.*

"That's so. That's so," Fattler said. "But I'm not

sure I'll be able to find it."

"But this is where you keep your safe. I know because I used to work here. It must be in the safe."

Fattler was anxious. "That's an interesting speech, isn't it?" he said.

Fern was breathing as silently as possible, trying not to make the slightest sound.

"Oh, yes. Great to be rid of the big burdens. Great relief to just be ordinary." He smiled. "You'll have to hurry here so you don't miss much more of it. The most important part is still to come!"

"Until I met Ubuleen, I never knew how ordinary I was," Fattler said. Fern glanced at Howard. Fattler wasn't ordinary!

"The safe, Mr. Fattler," the Somebody said. "Let's not waste time."

"Ah, yes," Fattler said. He walked toward Fern and Howard, who shrank back. He got closer and closer, until he was so close that he could have touched them. And then he turned and his eyes caught Fern's eyes, and then Howard's. Fern was ready to be ratted out, hauled through the lobby, delivered to the Bone and her grandmother. But Fattler didn't blink. He didn't show any sign that he'd seen them. He turned to the Somebody very calmly. "Have you tried our duck sauce recently?"

"Mr. Fattler, there's no time to discuss duck sauce."

"Right. Here we go." Then, as if he hadn't seen them at all, Fattler put one hand on the wall, and it sprouted a combination and the outline of the door to a safe. He began fiddling with the lock. "Ubuleen Heet would love our *blue cream* sauce. We call it the blue cream sauce. It's quite good, uses red wine that turns color in the process."

Blue cream? Fern thought. Didn't he just emphasize the words "blue cream"? He knows. He knows that Ubuleen Heet is the Blue Queen. *He's giving us a clue,* Fern thought. *He's letting us know that he knows.*

"It's written up in *Willy Fattler's Underground Hotel Cookbook*," Fattler said. "It's available for twenty-four ninety-nine, wherever Anybody books are sold."

"I'll let her know," the Somebody said.

The door to the safe opened and Fattler sighed, reaching in and rummaging. "It's a real mess in here." And then he jumped back. "Heavens!" A mouse jumped onto Fattler's lapel and scurried down his pants. The mouse darted down the row, past Howard and Fern. It was white with big long teeth that shone brightly. It was a strange mouse, really.

"Was that a mouse? What kind of a place are you running here?" the Somebody asked.

"Don't tell anyone," Fattler said. "Here," he said, holding up the key. "I've got it right here!" Fattler held up a shiny ivory key—sharp, long and white. It was connected to a small metal ring, and Fattler jingled it.

"I've never really had a handle on this place. I've really come to rely *on the Brain and the Brainkeeper*, and I owe that to Ubuleen. She's taught me many things."

Fern glanced at Howard. *The Brain! And the Brainkeeper?* Howard shrugged. He wasn't following either. Had Ubuleen already hypnotized Fattler? But wasn't he trying to tell her something?

"Excellent," said the Somebody, slipping the key

into his breast pocket. "Let's get back to the speech. I'd hate for you to miss out."

"I'll just hide out in the back," Fattler said. "I don't want to interrupt her. I'll *find a hiding place* and stick with it. Now let's hurry!" He looked at Fern and Howard one more time, a knowing gaze, and he repeated himself. "*Just find a hiding place.*" And then he walked out of the room with the Somebody.

Once they were gone, Howard let out a giant sigh and then panted a bit. "I was holding my breath. I almost passed out," he said. "We got lucky. He didn't tell on us."

"I wonder why he didn't," Fern said. She stood up and walked to the back of the aisle.

"What are you looking for?" Howard asked.

"That strange mouse," she said. "That very strange mouse."

"Why?" Howard asked. "Just let it go. I don't like mice."

"Willy Fattler is a genius. This magnificent hotel. Ever-changing. It's amazing," Fern said. "And we all have gifts. You have gifts, Howard, that aren't at all ordinary! That's what's wrong with being ordinary! It doesn't exist!" (Since I went to the Alton School for the Remarkably Giftless as a child, I often wonder about this. Were my teachers wrong, telling all the students there that we didn't have any gifts, that we couldn't create a gift of our own even if we rubbed two gifts

183

together? The more I get to know Fern, the more I'm sure that they were wrong. And the more I get to know people in the world—readers, you know, like you, who sometimes write me letters about your own amazing lives, sometimes quiet lives, sometimes rowdy lives, but always full, complicated lives—I start to think that nobody is truly ordinary, like Fern said. Not if you look hard enough. I've come to believe that we all have our own gifts—strange and lovely and true.)

"Wasn't it strange that he didn't tell on us," Fern said. "That he mentioned the *blue cream* sauce, and that when he reached for the key, a mouse darted out of the safe. How would a mouse get into a safe? He then talked about a hiding place and said to hurry, and then he looked at us. At us! Like he was trying to tell us something."

Fern saw the mouse now, squatting by a honey jar. Howard walked up beside her. "It is strange," he said. "And why does that mouse only have one giant tooth in the front, huh? See it?"

Fern did see it now: one long white shiny tooth. "Looks like ivory," Fern said. "Like the key that Fattler gave that guy."

"It does," Howard said.

"What if it *is* the key?" Fern said. "What if he grabbed the key and transformed it into this mouse and then transformed something else into the fake key that he handed over?"

184

"Could he do that?"

"He's a genius," Fern said. She knelt down and held out her hand. The mouse skittered toward her. It sniffed her hand and then clamored up into her palm. Fern petted its fur. Once, twice, and then on the third pet, the mouse grew harder, stiffer. Its fur disappeared, and its long singular front tooth thickened, and lengthened, until it took over the mouse's entire body. The mouse was gone and Fern was holding the key—the key to the castle.

Now they heard some noises coming from the other side of the lobby door again, and then some by the back door that they'd come through. "I haven't wanted to tell you this," Fern said. "But we're going to battle the Blue Queen. Tonight. At midnight."

"What?" Howard said. "We can't."

"We can and we will. And we don't have much time. This place isn't safe."

"How can we get out? They're at both doors."

"I think there might be another door. To the Brain."

Howard looked panic-stricken—worse than when he was hooked up in Mrs. Fluggery's coatroom, worse than on the elevator, worse than under the bed, worse than being chased by angry maids, worse than being British.

"I can't do this, Fern!" Howard screeched. "I want to go back!"

"We can't go back!"

"I have to," Howard said. "I can't go on. I'll sit on

this chair. I'll let them take me away. Gravers Military Academy! Fine! I can't face the Blue Queen, Fern! I won't!" Howard was gripping the sides of the chair, staring at the floor. Fern had never seen him this way. He was shaking his head. He looked hysterical.

"We've got to go forward," Fern said. "Together."

"No."

"We've got the key. We have to hide it! Fattler told us to!"

"No."

"What time is it?" she asked. The voices seemed so close now.

"Almost eight o'clock," Howard said. "Why?"

"We have time. But I still don't know where the meeting is. And how do I get to the Brain? Will it know anything? Midnight is when it begins."

"It begins? The battle?" Howard was shaking. His mouth was still forming the word "battle," over and over.

"I'm sorry," Fern said.

"You should be sorry. Wait! Sorry about what?" Howard asked.

"Sorry about this," she said, putting her hand on his shoulder. She gripped the key in her hand so tightly that its little teeth dug into her palm. She focused on Howard, though she wasn't sure what she wanted him to turn into. Something small, that she could carry with her, light, hollow. Something that she could hide a key inside.

"Sorry about *what*?" Howard said.

She shoved the key into his pocket.

"Fern?" His voice was becoming a soft, high, distant echo. "Fern? I don't feel quite right."

Fern watched him go pale. He slumped in his seat or maybe he wasn't slumping as much as he was actually smaller than before. He then began shrinking quickly. His skin took on a shine; his face plumped and then went snouty. He was sitting on the wooden chair in the size and shape of a pig.

But he wasn't a live pig. No. He was ceramic and pink with a slit on his back.

In other words, he was a piggy bank.

The applause in the other room soared, complete with hoots and shouts, as if this were what they'd been waiting for all along.

"Howard?" Fern whispered. She felt guilty. "I'm so sorry." His face still had a certain Howardlike expression, his look of shock frozen on his now piggy face. "Howard, I hate to tell you, but I've had to transform you. You're now a piggy bank. And you're hiding the key. I mean it's inside you. You were hysterical. I couldn't have gone on with you in that state. Plus I needed a hiding place for the key."

He didn't respond. He couldn't. He was a piggy bank, after all.

Fern then shook him gently. The key rattled inside,

along with something that was a little heavier. Maybe the Correct-O-Cure spray samples that had been in his pocket? Fern wasn't sure, although he smelled faintly of burnt plastic, and she didn't want to mention it. It wouldn't be funny in any way to Howard that the Correct-O-Cure samples were now lodged inside his new form, where he wouldn't be able to use the spray to try to reverse the situation, and Fern knew it wouldn't work anyway.

"It'll be okay," she told him, even though she was pretty sure that it wouldn't be. She tucked the piggy bank under her arm and headed back toward where she figured the door might be. She thought that she should go forward to some new place, soldier onward. It was the only way.

She'd reached into paintings before, sure, but never into a wall. She walked over to the spot where she'd seen the bee crawl out of the hole. The bee had come from a keyhole. Something had to be on the other side! She knew it wasn't a real wall; it was undercover. It had been hiding the safe, so it might also be hiding the way to the Brain. But still she was hesitant. She shoved; the wall gave. And just as the wall had sprouted a safe, it now sprouted a doorknob. This one was trembling so hard that it made her hand feel buzzy and itchy—a buzzing knob in her buzzing hand.

PART 4

THE BRAIN

THIS WAY TO THE BRAIN

WHEN FERN OPENED THE DOOR, SHE FOUND A narrow passageway, but it wasn't what she'd expected. It didn't have, for example, a well-crafted floor covered in shag carpeting, or wood-paneled walls like a normal passageway. No. It seemed carved out of rock and dirt and, well, geological matter. If I were a geologist and you were a geologist and we were just chatting amongst ourselves at a geology convention, I would use catchy geology catchphrases like "lithologically distinct" and "schistose sequences" and "calcite marble." But I'm not and you're not and we're not. So, I'm just hoping that you have kept it in your head that they were in Willy Fattler's *Underground* Hotel, and that this hotel exists under New York City. It's okay if you've let that slip from your mind for a while. Fern herself was so caught up in the fancy glam of flying monkeys and modern art that she was very surprised to find a passageway carved out of dirt and rock. But she was relieved to see that she'd found herself one step closer to the Brain. There was a small, crude arrow painted on the wall, with one word painted below it: BRAIN.

This is what Fattler had been talking about. The Brain and the Brainkeeper. Fern wanted to know if the Brain was really brainy. Did it know, for example, that

Ubuleen Heet was the Blue Queen? Did it know that Merton Gretel wasn't dead? Did it know the where-abouts of the rest of Merton Gretel's soul? Would it know that Howard held the key and would it know what the key could open?

With Howard-as-a-piggy-bank tucked under her arm, she walked down the passageway.

The passageway is hard to explain. It was dank and dimly lit with more bare bulbs. In this way, it was simple. But the passageway had a feel to it that was charged. There was the electric charge of the buzzing—but it was more than that. There was an electricity in the air that was foreign to Fern. It wasn't like anyplace she'd ever been before, not even the city beneath the city or the hotel or the stuffy storage room. Although it was made of rock, it seemed flimsy in a way that Fern couldn't put her finger on. It seemed like it barely existed—more imagined than real.

Fern was still haunted by that moment when she'd thought that she herself was being stored in a box, her own face swimming up to the surface of that mirror. She was scared; the passageway encouraged fear. She told herself that there was nothing to be scared of, but she didn't really believe that. It was the kind of thing she'd have told Howard just minutes before, and now he was made of ceramic and had a snout! She was sorry

193

about that, but she'd had to do it. Every once in a while she would say this to Howard, "Sorry, Howard. Really, but it had to be done."

The ground was uneven. Fern steadied herself with one hand on the passageway's cool, damp wall. Soon the passageway began to turn, left and right and left again. It tilted upward and there were crude steps—grooves, really, in the rock. Fern followed the steps, which only got steeper and steeper.

At one point she heard applause again, a distant uproar amid the deep buzz of the passageway. Ubuleen Heet's speech wasn't over. Her voice seemed to be coming from under Fern's feet. Fern assumed that the passageway led over the amphitheater. Ubuleen Heet's voice was just a distant warbling. She couldn't understand the words. But she could tell that the audience loved her. Ubuleen had them chanting something over and over. Fern wasn't sure what it was. *Encase your critter's meaty opacity? Emblaze your rimmer middle oglevary?* What was an oglevary? Then it came to her: *Embrace your inner mediocrity!* That was what Ubuleen was preaching! Mediocrity? Hugging the truly lackluster parts of yourself? So it wasn't just Fattler she was after. She didn't want anyone to strive. She didn't want anyone to try to be better versions of themselves. She wanted people to give up and be happy about it.

But why? Fern thought. Because it was easier to conquer other people if they didn't think too highly of themselves, starting with Willy Fattler. Because she wanted to get at their souls? Is that what the Secret Society of Somebodies was about?

"We're missing the speech," she told Howard-as-a-piggy-bank. "There's one thing we have going for us!" She kept climbing and winding along the passageway unsteadily.

The applause rang out from the amphitheater. She didn't want to hear people cheering for the Blue Queen. She sprinted jaggedly, the buzz building all around her. She ran hard, up and up until she was finally out of breath. When she came to a landing, she took a break. She put Howard-as-a-piggy-bank down on the step ahead of her and sat with a sigh. She wished that she could ask Howard what time it was. She had no idea how long she'd been climbing. Time seemed to have slipped away from everything. Had it been minutes? Hours?

She looked in the direction she'd come. At first she was confused. She'd traveled up one narrow passageway. But now when she looked down there were three, all leading to her spot on the stairs. She looked up.

There was only one passageway ahead of her. This seemed strange. How could she have not noticed that three passageways came together at this spot? She picked up Howard and again climbed the stairs. She was in just one passageway, as she'd been before. But when she looked back again, the three passageways seemed to have followed her.

Now she started to panic. It was one thing to walk into a single passageway. She'd known that she would always be able to just turn around, if she needed to, and go back the way she came. But now how would she know which of the three passageways behind her was the right passageway, the one that had lead her here?

Fern's heart started beating fast. She climbed again, faster this time, running and tripping and running some more. And when she looked back there were five passageways staring up at her, no longer just three.

She ran again, and quickly turned. This time there were ten passageways.

And the walls began to shift ever so slightly. Small black long beads rose up from the walls, but they weren't beads. They had legs, and fine hairs. They were black with a greenish shine.

Caterpillars.

They were caterpillars, and the high-pitched chorus of their voices rose. They roved the walls, and one dropped from above, landing on Fern's shoulder. "Thank you, Fern," it whispered. "Thank you for saving us!"

"I didn't save you," Fern said. "I don't know you."

"Where do caterpillars come from, Fern? How are we born? And how will we find our many ways home?"

These caterpillars weren't ordinary caterpillars. They could speak and think, and they had a certain shine to them, nearly a glow. And then Fern remembered that she'd learned once that caterpillars are born from eggs. "Eggs?" she asked quietly, and she thought of the egg-shaped pills, the souls that the Blue Queen had compressed, the ones Fern had stolen and then scattered by accident.

The caterpillar inched down her arm to the rock below. "Thank you!"

Fern watched the caterpillars as they slipped out of cracks in the passageway—the ground beneath and the walls on either side. They were scrabbling quickly toward her.

Fern grabbed Howard-as-a-piggy-bank and pushed herself away from the caterpillars. Were they souls? How was it possible? Fern supposed that the Blue Queen got her power from eating souls, and then she could store the ones she'd need for later—store them in this form. But Fern had set them loose when she broke the jars. What would happen to them now?

Fern ran up the grooved stairs, up and up and up. Each time she looked back, the passageways behind her had multiplied, and, within each passageway, there were more passageways to be seen. She'd never find her way back, so she kept running. The caterpillars became a far-off echo, and the buzzing grew louder and louder, until she could feel it vibrating in her own chest.

But then she heard the tune. It was the same tune that her invitation to the Secret Society of Somebodies meeting had played. It was coming from her pocket, just as it had the last time. She didn't want to open her pocket. She didn't want any more messages from the Blue Queen.

The tune was growing louder in her sweatshirt pocket, more insistent. It was an awful song, strung along on what now seemed to be a sickly melody. How could it have gotten there? She looked down at her pocket. It was baggy and stretched out. She remembered the man that she'd run into at the corner of the hotel, the Somebody who'd held on to her by her pocket and then, for no reason at all, seemed to just let her go. Had he put something in there?

Fern peeked in the pocket and then slowly opened it. There was the sharp corner of an invitation. She pulled out the envelope, opened it and unfolded a gold-trimmed piece of paper. It had four words written on it: SDOOF KROY WEN. HURRY!

Another mystery? She didn't want another mystery.

She was lost. She didn't know what time it was. She had to hurry, of course. But she didn't know where she was hurrying to. What help was it to tell her to hurry! She was sure that she was failing. She thought of her grandmother and the Bone, how worried they must be.

She'd come too far to chicken out.

Fern put Howard-as-a-piggy-bank down beside her. She looked at the gold-trimmed piece of paper with the mysterious SDOOF KROY WEN written on it, and this time Fern wasn't impressed. She didn't care about the gold trim. She didn't care about how fancy the Secret Society of Somebodies sounded. She didn't want to be royal, not really. No. She didn't want to have to go on and prove to her grandmother that she could do it, that she didn't need her grandmother's help as the Great Realdo. She looked down at the apple in her pocket. She didn't care about making history. What did she really want? She wanted to be a daughter. She wanted to know what her mother would tell her at a moment like this. She closed her eyes and cupped her hands to her mouth. She whispered, "Was I made royalty too soon? Am I not ready for this? Should I just go home?" Tears began to roll down her face and collected at her chin. "I'm scared," she said. "I don't think I can do it."

She listened for a moment and then let her hands slip to her lap. Her mother was dead. Her mother's voice was gone. She was alone.

And then there wasn't so much a voice as there were words, a string of them playing in her mind, and Fern knew that her mother was answering her. *The world is always changing, but there's a part of you that never changes. It's essentially you, and you can always rely on it to be true.*

Fern knew that her mother was right. There was something about Fern herself that was true and unchanging. It was good and strong, and she could rely on it. Couldn't she? Even now after everything that had gone wrong? Fern remembered what Howard had said while he was trying to spray the burnt-plastic-scented Correct-O-Cure on his beans. *Everyone has to have faith in something.* And Hyun-Arnold had told her something like that too, hadn't he? He'd lost his accent completely and said, *You've really got to be yourself in this life. You have to rely on something deep inside.* It had seemed like a contradiction at the time, coming from him, but now it seemed like it fit with all the others.

"I'll fix this, Howard," Fern promised, scooping him up. She'd have to keep Howard safe. She'd have to find this place called SDOOF KROY WEN and face the Blue Queen and do her best. "I'll find a way," she said.

She stood and looked down through the passageways—more and more passageways every moment. And then she ran the other way. She ran up and up until she was breathless and had come to a door, a single, enormous door with a sign on it, a sign jiggling fiercely with vibrations. It read YOU ARE HERE. WELCOME TO THE BRAIN!

THE BRAINKEEPER

FERN KNOCKED ON THE DOOR.

No one answered.

She looked down at Howard-as-a-piggy-bank and his permanently shocked face. Fern knocked again, and again there was no answer. She eyed the walls, on the lookout for caterpillars. She fiddled with the gold-trimmed paper in her pocket and tapped the apple with her fingernails. She tried not to look at the passage-ways, which were still silently multiplying behind her. She had no idea which one she'd come from, but it didn't seem to matter anymore. She wasn't going back.

She banged again on the door, this time with the butt of her fist and all of her might.

A whistle sounded out—three short, shrill notes. The buzzing whirred down to a low constant hum. A man's gruff voice shouted from the other side of the oversized door, "Who's there, hmmm? Hmmm? Who is it?" And then the voice hooted owlishly for a bit, and stopped.

"My name is Fern," Fern shouted through the door. "I'm looking for the Brain. Maybe I'm lost."

"You're either lost or you know where you are. Do you know where you are?"

"I'm at a door that's got a sign that says, 'You are here. Welcome to the Brain!'" Fern said.

The door whipped open, creating a momentary breeze, but no one was standing on the other side. It seemed to have opened on its own.

Fern stood in the huge empty rectangle where the door used to be, and she found herself facing a giant machine that filled the giant room. The machine had long arms and shafts and conveyor belts that reached the high ceiling. Its massive body was made of gears and levers and typewriter keys and ancient adding machines and spinning fan belts and multiple motors. At the moment the machine was still. None of its parts were moving. Spools of thin, white paper—narrow as a fortune in a cookie, but unending—had spilled out of various slots throughout the machine and curled like ribbon in heaps on the floor. Small mirrors were positioned in and around the machine, giving angled views on its underparts and greasy innards. Fern thought back to the storage room, and it made sense that this machine would require all of those things down there, including the motor oil and the box of mirrors—all except, perhaps, the honey jars. And there was something else, too, that Fern noticed. Although the machine wasn't on at the moment, there was still this humming buzz. It wasn't as loud as it had been, but it was still there, a constant static. Fern tilted up Howard's piggy-bank face so that he could get the whole view, in case he was still able to see through his ceramic eyes.

"Well, well, then, you know exactly where you are and so you are not lost!"

Fern had nearly forgotten about the voice, she was so taken by the hulking machine. She looked around in hopes of finding someone, but no one was there. She noticed now that there was a cot, a desk, a sofa with a rug, a minikitchen, and a door that must have led to a bathroom. It was a large factory-sized room with a row of smoked-over windows too grimy to see through. In faint, chipped paint above the windows was the sign HURLMAN AND SISTERS GLASS ELEVATOR FACTORY. It was the old factory that the elevator operator had mentioned. Fern pivoted this way and that. "Are you the Brain?" Fern called out, peering around.

A head popped up—a man with small, round glasses and a bit of an overbite, so that you could see his front teeth even though he wasn't smiling. He was, in fact, frowning bitterly. But this wasn't the actual man. It was only a reflection in a mirror, and so Fern tried to trace the reflection to a real head, but she found only a reflection of the head again in another mirror, and again and again. The head kept appearing in mirrors and disappearing from them.

Finally the voice was right next to Fern. "I'm not the Brain. I'm the Brainkeeper."

When Fern turned, the man was standing right next to her. "Oh," she said, surprised. "You're here."

There were some things about this man, this brainkeeper, that were fairly normal. He was wiping his grease-stained fingers on an old rag, which is normal for someone who works with machinery. He wore suspenders, which is normal for someone missing the necessary backside to keep up a pair of pants. He wore a silver whistle on a string around his neck, which is normal for a, well, for a gym coach. But even though he was a small, nonathletic Brainkeeper with a brittle little caved-in chest, this wasn't too very strange. Obviously he used the whistle to operate the on-and-off of the machine, much like the big whistle that had probably sat atop Hurlman and Sisters Glass Elevator Factory a long time ago.

The thing that was not at all normal about this Brainkeeper was this: He was abuzz, and the reason he was abuzz was because his arms were covered in bees. At first glance one might think, well, this is just a Brainkeeper with very furry arms who happens to like to hum in a deep register. But, no, you would be wrong. He stood there with his hands on his hips, and his arms were alive with bees crawling all over one another.

"And you're here too!" he said.

"I know," Fern said, trying not to stare at the bees. (It's usually impolite to stare at someone's oddity.) She assumed that the bees weren't stinging him, because he was wearing a wry smile now.

"And you're not lost," he said, almost cheerfully. "This is the Brain!" He pointed to the giant machine, as if that explained everything.

There was a giant clock on the wall. She'd lost a lot of time in the passageway. It was 11:27—only thirty-three minutes to midnight! "Um, well, I need help. I'm supposed to be somewhere else. Very soon. I'm almost out of time."

"I can't help you get somewhere else. I'm not from around here. I only know this room. I only know this machine!" He stared at the machine like it was his greatest enemy. "Let me explain how this baby works—"

"Um, I don't really have a lot of time. I have some questions. . . ."

The Brainkeeper ignored her. "Well, I was contracted to build the Brain to help Fattler keep up with all his work. He isn't a genius like we thought, you see. He's ordinary. Ubuleen Heet enlightened him. And so the Brain is necessary to keep all his transformations going. Do you think Fattler's Underground Hotel works all by itself? It can't possibly! And since Fattler obviously can't do it, someone's got to keep it going and keep it all straight! Perfectly, perfectly straight!" The Brain-keeper's face crinkled up as if he'd smelled something sour. He paced a circle. "Perfectly straight . . . not so muddled!" He scratched his head in a befuddled way, and then lifted the silver whistle from his chest and blew into it, holding a note for three seconds.

Before Fern knew it, the elaborate machinery started up. It buzzed and ticked and clacked. It jittered and wheezed and rattled. From various locations, it spit out ticker tape—long strands of paper with small words and numbers written on them. In its herky-jerky motion, the contraption reminded Fern of the Bone's old jalopy—though the jalopy was just a very small contraption by comparison—and she suddenly missed her father deeply. Although she didn't miss school, not in the least, and although she was happy not to be doing Mrs. Fluggery's twenty pages of home-work, she did miss home, and she did miss Howard being Howard with all his Howard ways.

The Brain belched small puffs of smoke up into the air, as if the machine were smoking cigars. The Brainkeeper had scurried away from Fern while she wasn't looking, and now he was on his hands and knees crawling on the floor while staring up at some parts under the machinery that were puffing away.

Fern caught up with him. He was a very quick crawler, and he was hard to keep up with. "I've got an emergency," Fern explained loudly. "I need help!"

"So what?" the Brainkeeper shouted. "Everyone needs help!" Then he corrected himself, "Except me! I don't need any help!" The bees on his arms took on the shape of muscles as the Brainkeeper beat a pipe with a wrench again and again, then pouted.

"Is something wrong?" Fern shouted.

The Brainkeeper stood up and put his hands on his hips. "I used to be a beekeeper, if you can imagine that."

Fern nodded with a shrug. She could imagine that, quite easily.

"But there isn't much money in honey. I even went into bee training!" On cue, the bees formed a top hat on his head, leaving the Brainkeeper's skinny arms bare. "But there isn't much money in that either. So when I got the call to set up a system here for Mr. Fattler, well, I had to say yes."

"Who called you?" Fern asked.

"Miss Heet, of course. She's Fattler's counsel. She's taking care of him. She told me that I could do it. She can be very persuasive."

Fern huffed. "Has this Brain ever worked?"

"My grandfather warned me that I should stick to what I know. But no, no. I had to go and believe that building a brain and a hive weren't so different. Turns out"—he let his hand run over his bee beard and spoke to his bees—"he warned us, didn't he, my little engines?"

Fern was fairly sure that the Brainkeeper was crazy. She was embarrassed for him—a grown man talking to bees. She looked at the clock again. She was losing time. Why had Hyun-Arnold given her this clue? The Brain! Some help.

He stared at Fern. "You've got your piggy bank there, full of money, no doubt. You don't know what it's like to only eat honey, day after day. I can't go back! I've got to make this work!" He grabbed a handful of ticker tape. "It's supposed to track every transformation in this hotel! This is gobbledygook! Junk! Nothing!" He stomped over to another section. "You're supposed to be able to put a question in this slot here. It runs through the machine and spits out its answer here." He pointed at another slot.

Fern pulled out the invitation. "I have a question!" Fern said. "Could we test it?"

The Brainkeeper put his hands to his face. The bees formed a shawl over his shaking shoulders. Was he crying? He wiped his face, and red-eyed, bleary, he said, "It won't work. I'm a fake! A failure!"

"Let's just try it," Fern said. She took a piece of paper from his desk and scribbled on it: *Where is* SDOOF KROY WEN? *How do I get there?* Then she slipped it into the first slot.

The question zipped and twanged and bulleted and popped all around the Brain and then zipped back again.

"That part was good!" Fern said. "Impressive!"

The Brainkeeper shook his head. The machine spit out the piece of paper on his shoes.

Fern didn't have to pick it up. She could see that no answer had been written on it. The piece of paper was just as she'd written it. She could see herself holding Howard, and the Brainkeeper next to her, crawling in bees, reflected in the many mirrors in various spots all over the Brain. They were a sad group. The clock on the wall read 11:46. Fourteen minutes to midnight. The Secret Society of Somebodies meeting was about to begin.

Fern had been through a lot. She'd been expelled. She'd jumped into a giant invitation and landed in a crazy elevator. She'd seen the Blue Queen swallow bits of souls from books. She'd nearly had her own soul taken. She'd lost bits of souls from cracked jars. She'd turned herself into a dog and Howard, her near-brother, into a piggy bank. She'd run through a terrible passageway and talked to caterpillars, and now she was here. It was all so overwhelming, and now, the Brain—the one thing she thought would help—was useless.

And then her eyes settled on one of the many mirrors attached to the machinery, and there was her piece of paper, but this time it was reflected in the mirror and so it was backward. It read, quite plainly: ИƎW YOЯK ꟻOOꟼƧ.

3

CHAOS BELOW!

NEW YORK FOODS! IT HAD BEEN SO SIMPLE. YOU probably figured it out right away, because you're astonishingly (almost freakishly) bright. We should give Fern a break for not figuring it out. Remember she was under great stress—the caterpillars, the multiplying passageways, that odd Brainkeeper and his ever-rearranging bees! But did you see *this* coming: surly flying monkeys? An allergic reaction? Fire? Chaos? Mayhem? I bet you didn't! Fern certainly had no idea. But it's all on its way.

Also, New York Foods—is it any less mysterious forward than it is backward? Not a whole lot!

"Where is this place?" Fern asked the Brainkeeper.

The Brainkeeper said, "I bet it's in New York and has something to do with the sale of food items."

"Thanks," Fern said. The Brainkeeper had a gift for the obvious.

"I wouldn't suggest trying to find it by going back the way you've come."

"How do we get out of here?" Fern asked.

"What you need is a back door."

"Do you have one?"

"Nope."

"Or a way of shooting out that row of old windows and making your way to the ground safely."

"Is that possible?"

"Nope."

"What you need is a glass elevator."

Fern didn't want to ask again, but she had little choice. "Do you have one of those?"

"Sure!" the Brainkeeper said. "Just push one of those buttons there."

Well, there it was: a panel with two plastic buttons, one with an up arrow and one with a down arrow. There didn't seem to be an elevator door, but Fern took this in stride. The last elevator she'd been in had dropped her off inside a snowy wardrobe. Fern ran over and hit the button.

But this seemingly quiet moment—Fern and Howard-as-a-piggy-bank awaiting the glass elevator—is when things began to go crazy. And the craziness began with a knock on the door. A high-pitched voice shouted out, "Housekeeping!"

Fern didn't trust the voice. "Don't answer it!" she said. "Just wait till I get out of here."

"We're a bit out of the way, you know," he said to Fern. "That elevator might take a while."

"How long?"

"Hard to say."

Fern held on to Howard-as-a-piggy-bank tightly. She muttered, "Hard to say. We have an emergency." She pushed the button again, as if this would help hurry the elevator along.

The Brainkeeper headed for the door himself this time, his bees arranged as a lapel with a huge corsage on his overalls. "I've got to open the door. If I didn't, people would think that there's something wrong up here with the Brain."

"Something is wrong with the Brain!"

"Shhh," the Brainkeeper said. "I shouldn't have told you that!"

"Don't open the door!" Fern said, but the Brainkeeper wasn't listening. Fern feared that Fattler, Dorathea and the Bone, and the Blue Queen herself were at the door. She squatted with Howard-as-a-piggy-bank behind the old sofa. But as it turned out, it was none of these.

215

Instead there were two women in gray uniforms bustling into the room. Fern recognized them straightaway. The one like a wrestler was pushing a cleaning cart with a bum wheel; the other with her exploded bun was pushing an upright vacuum cleaner. It was of course the maids who'd chased them out of Ubuleen Heet's room.

"Housekeeping!" the exploded-bun maid said in an anxious scream.

"Do you have to clean right now?" the Brainkeeper asked.

"Yes!" the wrestler maid shouted. "Everything's gone strange down there! The flying monkeys are scaring everyone to death! Circling, eyeing everyone like hawks," she said with a shiver. "They've gone bad, I tell you. They're on the hunt!"

"On the hunt for what?" the Brainkeeper asked.

"Don't know! They just circle and sometimes haul someone away. It's awful. Everyone's running off. It's chaos!"

"What else can we do but clean?" said the wrestler maid, pulling out her Windex with a shaky hand. "It's what we're paid for."

"Where's Fattler?" the Brainkeeper asked, panic-stricken.

"Gone!" the wrestler maid and exploded-bun maid said in unison, staring blankly like lost children.

"Gone where?" the Brainkeeper asked.

They shrugged.

"You should know. Doesn't that contraption know everything?" the exploded-bun maid asked.

"Who's in charge?" the Brainkeeper asked.

"Flying monkeys," the exploded-bun maid said, nervously folding ticker tape. "Haven't you been listening?"

"But," the wrestler maid said with a smile, "we did finally catch what we've been looking for!"

"This!" said the exploded-bun woman, pulling something from the pocket of her gray uniform, something white and wriggling, and, well, hoofed.

Fern popped up from behind the sofa. "My pony!" Fern said.

"Your pony?" said the exploded-bun woman.

"Yes," Fern said. "He's made out of Mrs. Fluggery's hair," Fern said, even though this wouldn't make any sense to them.

"Here, then," the exploded-bun woman said. "You take him."

"I know you," the wrestler maid said as if something terrible had just gotten worse. "You're one of them stowaways!" She shoved the pony at Fern.

"I was invited here," Fern said.

The wrestler woman said, "See"—she turned to the Brainkeeper—"more trouble. Stowaways getting invited here! It makes no sense!"

Fern held the pony tight to her ribs. It was so good to see him again. It was as if she'd forgotten that she'd ever been in normal school with Mrs. Fluggery's Rules and Regulations. But now she had proof that she'd had another life, and she wanted to get back to it—back to the Bone and Dorathea and Howard as Howard.

"Flying monkeys!" the Brainkeeper said. "They're no good when they turn evil!"

Fern held tight to Howard-as-a-piggy-bank. "I think I know what they're after," Fern said.

"What's that, hon?" the wrestler maid asked.

Fern ran to the elevator and pressed the buttons again and again. They lit up just as screeches echoed up the passageways. Monkey screeches.

FLYING MONKEYS TURNED EVIL

"LISTEN!" THE WRESTLER MAID SAID, HOLDING her breath, a bottle of Windex shaking in her hand.

"Furry foul creatures! They're coming!" The exploded-bun woman started crying while trying to sweep up a pile of endless ticker tape. "Don't look at them!"

"I won't!" the wrestler maid said.

The pony in one arm, Howard-as-a-piggy-bank in the other, Fern flattened herself against the wall next to the elevator buttons and slid down behind the sofa. "Hurry up," she said to the elevator. "Hurry, hurry!"

"No, no," the Brainkeeper said. "I'm not ready. I mean, if I could have just a few more weeks to get all the kinks out, to get this thing up to speed!" He stared at Fern. "They'll find me out! I'll be back to eating honey!"

A pair of flying monkeys swooped into the room through the open door. Their broad wings created an updraft. They were hairy, their wings leathery like those on bats. They stunk, too. They landed on the floor, dropped to all fours and started stalking the room.

"Hey!" the Brainkeeper said, the bees turning into a hat of various fruits on top of his head. "Good to see you!" The Brainkeeper tried to chat up one of the monkeys. "So, you're a monkey and you fly. Interesting."

The monkey scratched his armpit and waddled off, but the Brainkeeper followed him, keeping up his attempt at distracting banter.

The maids kept cleaning.

The other monkey was sniffing the air, his wide nostrils tensing. He walked toward Fern, who sat as still as possible. She closed her eyes. If she'd had them open, she would have noticed a bee crawling over Howard's hoof and up his leg. Howard, in his piggy-bank state, could feel the bee on his leg. He had sensations still, albeit weakened, and Howard was afraid of bees. He was allergic, remember?

And so it was bad timing really when the bee stung Howard, and Howard-as-a-piggy-bank let out a small squeal. It wasn't a true pig squeal—he was still ceramic—but it was a squeal nonetheless. The flying monkey flapped up and appeared above Fern, his talons on the back of the sofa, his wings beating to keep his balance. His foul scent pressed down on Fern. He lowered his head toward her. Howard's piggy bank leg was swelling, the ceramic skin getting shinier and shinier. The flying monkey was so close now, she could feel his breath on her face.

"He's been stung. He needs ice," Fern said. "He's allergic. He's swelling up."

The flying monkey didn't seem to care. He flapped his wings angrily and screeched. The other monkey rushed over, the Brainkeeper running after him.

"Don't look!" the exploded-bun maid shouted.

"I don't see a thing!" the wrestler maid said.

Fern was surrounded by beating wings and screeching.

"They want your money," the Brainkeeper said. "Give it to them!"

"It's not my money," Fern said, letting go of the pony and holding Howard-as-a-piggy-bank as tightly as she could.

The Brainkeeper ran to her and pulled on Howard. "Give them what they want!" he shouted.

"No!" Fern said. She kicked the Brainkeeper in the shins. The bees were sailing off the Brainkeeper because of the gusty wind kicked up by the leathery, foul-smelling wings. The buzzing bee wings roared.

"Don't look!" the maids were shouting to each other. "Close your eyes!"

Fern could barely see through the haze of bees, but the Brainkeeper had a good grip on the piggy bank.

"There are things more important than money!" he said.

"I know!" Fern shouted back.

The Brainkeeper was wiry but strong and, with the wind and bees, Fern couldn't help but lose her grip. One of the flying monkeys snatched Howard-as-a-piggy-bank, and the two flapped to the high factory windows. The one without Howard-as-a-piggy-bank crashed through

first, glass raining down. The other monkey followed, gripping Howard-as-a-piggy-bank, and flapping out into the dark night.

Fern turned to the Brainkeeper angrily. "That was my friend!" she said.

"Money is no friend," the Brainkeeper said. "I'd rather eat only honey and have one good friend than be stuck here alone!"

"You are stuck here alone, day in and day out!"

The Brainkeeper stared around. "Oh."

"And that piggy bank was Howard, a boy. A boy in the shape of a piggy bank. And if the Brain worked, you'd know that!"

"Oh."

The maids opened their eyes. The exploded-bun maid looked at the broken glass. "That's a mess."

"It sure is," the wrestler maid said.

"Is that all you two can worry about?" Fern looked at the clock. Four minutes to midnight. The Blue Queen's powers would be hitting their stride. "I'm in a real dire emergency here! I've got to battle the Blue Queen! Ubuleen Heet is the Blue Queen! She isn't Fattler's counselor! She's brainwashed him. He's just lost his confidence. She's got him believing he needs a Brain and a Brainkeeper! There are souls at stake! And, and, and . . ." Fern was breathless. "My friend has been carried away by flying monkeys who sniffed out the key that's hidden inside him! The key that will help the Blue Queen take over again!"

The two maids and the Brainkeeper stood in silence for a moment.

"Why didn't you say so from the get-go?" the Brainkeeper said.

"Well, we'd have surely helped," the wrestler woman said.

"As best we could've," the exploded-bun maid said.

"Oh, well then," Fern said.

Just then there was a loud *ding*, and elevator doors opened.

"I'm going to go try to fix things," Fern said. "Do you want to help?"

The Brainkeeper was suddenly distracted, calling his bees. "My little engines! Come to me! Come to me!" He had his arms held out. "I would, um. I certainly would, but . . ."

"Oh," the wrestler maid said, "we're needed. I mean without us, who would clean up that glass on the floor over there?"

The exploded-bun woman added, "And, well, we've punched in. You know, we're on the clock. So we couldn't possibly."

"Oh, I see," Fern said, disappointed. She walked to

the elevator. "Everyone should have faith in something, and I have faith in you all," she said, wishing it were true. "I'm not sure why. But I do, even though you haven't helped me and even though you've just said that you won't." She looked at each one. They stared at her. "I can't explain it," she said. "But I still have faith. It's the stubborn kind."

She hoped this would make them charge forward, but they didn't. They stood there somewhat ashamed of themselves and maybe a little indignant that Fern was asking for help, and feeling sorry for themselves too for being in such a position. All of this passed across their faces.

Fern stepped into the elevator. The doors shut. She gave a frustrated sigh.

"Floor, please!" a voice called out.

Fern turned, expecting to see the same elevator operator who'd taken her and Howard to the city beneath the city, sitting there in his cap and vest, fiddling with his pressurized buttons. But it wasn't the same operator. This one was young. His vest was loose and saggy around his spindly frame.

"I don't know what floor," Fern said. "All I know is New York Foods."

He nodded his head. "That's up above. It's a secret line. I've never used it."

"Where does the secret line lead to?" Fern asked.

"Inside the castle gazebo," the elevator operator said. "On the royal grounds. I've been wanting to see it. Is that where you want to go?"

Fern nodded. "As fast as you can," she said.

The elevator operator said, "Okay then!" He pushed a button, but the elevator didn't move. "Darn you, Charlie Horse!" the kid said.

"Hey," Fern said. "Did this elevator used to belong to an operator who wore a very tight vest?"

"That's right!" the young elevator operator said, fiddling with some buttons. "He up and quit. Just like that. He went off to take engineering lessons. Always wanted to design things like this, I guess."

Fern smiled to herself. He'd listened to her advice. Imagine that!

Just then a bell *ding*ed again. The elevator operator opened the door. "More passengers," he said.

And there stood the Brainkeeper and the two maids, blurry in a cloud of bees.

PART 5

THE SECRET SOCIETY
OF SOMEBODIES

THE GAZEBO

THE ELEVATOR OPERATOR GOT CHARLIE HORSE up and running. He threw it into high gear. They chugged up, up, up and swerved to one side then the other. They bucked and flew. Fern, the Brainkeeper and the two maids sank to the floor and braced themselves. Fern gripped the miniature humpbacked pony.

The elevator hoisted itself up to the surface of New York City, specifically into the chilly back room of New York Foods, to get on the right track. Through a thick pane of glass, Fern could see shoppers pushing carts, pawing tomatoes under fluorescent lights. On the top of the glass, she saw the etched words ƧᗡOOℲ ꓘЯOY WƎИ, which of course, when read by the shoppers on the other side of the glass, read NEW YORK FOODS. The elevator only hesitated here for a moment, just long enough to switch tracks, and then it plummeted back down to the city beneath the city. Fern's stomach rose to her throat. The maids held hands. The Brainkeeper talked to his bees, which had calmed quickly and were now arranged like medals of honor covering the chest of his overalls. "It's okay," he said. "Don't be frightened." But by the quaver in his voice, it was plain that he was frightened. Fern was frightened for Howard. She imagined him in the flying monkey's clutches, swooping through the open air. Fern wondered if she'd be able to save him.

The elevator popped up and stopped. It let out a *bing*! The door opened.

Fern and the others said good-bye to the young elevator operator and stepped out. They were inside the gazebo, near a quiet fishpond, the fishes' orange and gold bodies swishing in the light. Through the lattice, across the front lawn, they could see the meeting of the Secret Society of Somebodies. Circling a grassy mound lit with two tall torches were the members— hundreds of them, maybe even thousands. Instead of the more businessy blazers, they were now wearing robes of varying colors, with the Triple S emblem stitched where their lapels would have been. They were poised with their hands above their heads, not as if they were under arrest, but more like they were holding down the shoulders of a much taller foe. They hummed prayerfully.

Fern could see a hunkered form on the grassy mound. At first she wasn't sure what it was, but as she stared, it took shape.

"It's Fattler," the Brainkeeper said, his bees humming on his shirt.

Fattler was sitting in a chair. Ubuleen Heet stood beside him. She was in her motivational speaker mode—energetic but refined, her cocoon-and-moth brooch pinned to her white robe. The filigree clock on the spire was *gong*ing midnight.

"So, Willy, do you think we're here to celebrate your ordinary nature? To celebrate your freedom from the shackles of genius?"

Fattler sat back in the chair. "If that's the case, well then, that is awfully kind of you! It's unnecessary, though, because I'm really an ordinary guy now. Just me." He knew it wasn't why he was there. He'd been found out. The key. *She must have tried it on the door to the castle,* Fern thought. The Blue Queen looked angry—a pressured hatred that was boiling just below the surface. Fattler could feel it too—he had to. He was sweating. His eyes darted anxiously.

231

Fern searched the crowd for the flying monkeys. Had she beaten them there? She looked up through the lattice to see if they were on their way, flying above. She could see the castle's spire wedged into the dirty underside of New York City. She remembered how she'd pictured a family in Central Park having a picnic right above the castle's spire, not even the least bit aware of what was pointing at them from below. That family would be asleep in their beds now, and the spot above the spire empty and dark.

Behind the gazebo there were some food tables, picked over and abandoned. The exploded-bun woman pulled the tablecloth off each table like a magician. She threw one to each of them. "Robes," she said.

Fern caught hers and wrapped it around herself, making a knot near her shoulders.

The Brainkeeper pulled a pen out of his pocket and wrote "SSS" on his makeshift robe and passed it on.

The wrestler woman said, "We'll sneak in and mingle."

Fern was scared. Her thoughts felt jumbled. She was relieved when the wrestler woman said, "Look there," and pointed to a hedgerow. "You can hide behind that, follow it all the way to the front of the crowd."

"Good luck," the exploded-bun woman said.

The Brainkeeper smiled weakly. "I've never done anything like this before. I only know bees."

Fern had never done anything quite like this before either.

The Brainkeeper and the maids walked down and joined the crowd.

At this point Ubuleen was working up to her request. "For all that I have done for you, Willy Fattler, I asked only for one thing in return. Only one thing. And you gave me a fake!" She held the ivory key above her head. "What is it really, Fattler? Is it a—" She cupped the key in her hands and then opened them finger by finger to reveal a strand of pearls. The Blue Queen ripped the strand in half. The pearls went flying out, raining down on the heads of Somebodies, who didn't flinch or move. They only kept up their humming.

"Those belonged to my dear old auntie, who's dead now!" Fattler said. "I wish you hadn't done that."

"Oh, you'll wish I hadn't done a lot of things," the Blue Queen said.

"Wait," Fattler said. "How did you do that? I mean, you aren't supposed to have any powers, not after you were stripped of them after, you know, the past incident."

"Oh, stripped of my powers! The Great Realdo! And where is our Great Realdo now? Where is Dorathea? And her dear Mr. Bone?" The Blue Queen looked around as if truly mystified, and then she raised her finger in the air as if she just remembered something. "Lucess! Come here! Show them!"

Lucess was holding the fishbowl. Her father was swimming in it, but he wasn't alone. There were two other fish swimming in the bowl. One had enormous eyes that Fern recognized immediately—her grandmother. The other had blond eyelashes and ruddy cheeks—her father. Fern felt her whole body go cold. Dorathea and the Bone had been captured. They were stuck, like Merton Gretel, though they probably didn't even know they were stuck with Merton Gretel. They were just fish, spinning around in a bowl. They weren't coming to save Fern. Fern had to save them.

The Blue Queen went on. "I'm not stupid, Fattler. I didn't just get cast out and waste away! I had to get creative. Anybodies love books, you know. And why? Maybe because they transport us, transform us—and because we can make the imagined real. But also because those writers put their souls into those books they create, not even knowing it, probably—stupid writers! Imagine, we actually have access to their souls. And then Anybodies close the book and leave the soul there for the next reader, because it would be *too evil* to take it. *Too evil?* The writers left their souls behind. If they didn't want them stolen, they should have guarded them more closely!" the Blue Queen said. "So I started getting souls and power from books—fresh, strong souls. The first one took a lot of effort. My daughter had to help—dear girl!"

Fern spotted Lucess holding the fishbowl—her father swimming in it—standing near a trunk, filled with books, no doubt. She turned away and stared into the bowl. She was ashamed, Fern could tell. But her mother had made her do it, hadn't she? Fern felt sorry for her. "After that one gave me some power, I had enough to get the next. And with each one, I grew stronger and stronger. I had to work the nonexistent muscles of my Anybody powers back. Like someone who has to learn to walk again after a car crash."

Willy looked at her blankly. "You found a loop-hole."

"I did. I certainly did. And now I need that *key*!" Ubuleen Heet almost lost her temper. Her arms shook at her sides, but then Lucess spoke up from beside her. Fern couldn't hear what Lucess said, but the comment calmed her mother, for the moment. "All I want, Willy," she said, "is a key to the castle, so that I can properly be restored to my rightful place."

"I don't have the key," Willy said, standing up as if just to stretch his legs.

"You do!" Ubuleen Heet shouted.

"I don't know where it went," he said. "I think it ran off!"

"Ran off where, to whom?" Ubuleen asked.

He paused a moment and then shrugged his shoulders. "I don't remember," he said. And then his mouth twisted—was it a smile? "My ordinary brain doesn't hold facts all that well."

"Oh, it doesn't, does it?" Ubuleen said. She held both her arms up in the air. Her face took on a bluish glint in the torchlight. "Tie him down!" she yelled.

Two Somebodies charged up the mound and forced him back into the chair. He bent forward. His face in the torchlight was pinched and desperate. One of the Somebodies tied his hands tightly behind his back and rigged the rope to the chair.

"Don't try to break loose, Fattler. Or I will begin taking lives once again. And who knows who I'll start with this time!" The Blue Queen shouted, "Send up the souls!"

The crowd roared with shouts and applause.

Lucess pushed the trunk up the mound in front of Fattler's shiny black shoes. Lucess looked tired and weak. The trunk was heavy and, by the time she'd unlatched its lid and opened it up, she was breathless, but also wide-eyed and obviously scared.

Fern wasn't sure what to do. How could she possibly help? She didn't trust herself. What if she confronted the Blue Queen and couldn't control her powers? What if she could only turn the Blue Queen's hair into a pony—and not even know how she did it? What if her hands turned into books again, and this time she simply handed over her soul, bit by bit? Part of Fern wanted to turn back. What could she do with her measly powers?

But then she thought of Howard. Where was Howard? She'd gotten him into this mess. She thought of Merton Gretel, her grandmother's brother—his gills, his heart, his need for the rest of his soul. She thought of Lucess Brine. Poor Lucess. She deserved a good father after all she'd been through, a father who was able to really love her.

The miniature humpbacked pony wriggled in Fern's arms, restless as ever.

"Stop it," Fern said, frustrated. "Don't you know anything? This isn't the time for messing around."

But the pony seemed bent on something. He jumped from her arms. Fern watched him trot off toward the torchlight. She knew it was the right thing to do.

MORE SOULS

THE TRUNK WAS FILLED WITH BOOKS.

The Secret Society of Somebodies began to hum louder. Fern knew the tune quite well by now—the one from the invitation and the passageway. But now she could make out the words—"Hail the Blue Queen! Hail! Hail the Blue Queen." It was an anthem that now was picking up steam. The air was windy. The Blue Queen, standing behind Fattler, raised her thick blue arms. The trunk began to glow with the dusky light of the authors' souls that had been stitched into the books. Fern knew what was coming. She remembered it all, in terribly precise detail, from the time she'd looked on from underneath the bed: The Blue Queen was going to swallow pieces of souls.

Fern glanced around the crowd's feet for the minia-ture humpbacked pony, but she didn't see him. The two maids and the Brainkeeper had mixed in perfectly. Fern couldn't see them either. Although it made Fern feel weak in her knees, she inched through the hedges, closer and closer, until she could see Fattler's moist eyes, shining in the light beaming up from the bits of souls in the trunk.

Lucess's face was lit up too. She was stiff with fear.

The Blue Queen beckoned the souls, and the books flapped wildly in the box. The crowd cheered. They knew she was the Blue Queen. They'd known all along. The dusky, egg-shaped souls lifted up over Fattler's head, and into the mouth of the Blue Queen.

"No," Fattler said. "Stop this! You'll never get away with it!"

But the books were now being dragged from the trunk by the sheer force of the Blue Queen's will. Some of the books struggled. Fern was close enough, having made her way down the hedgerow, to read the titles. The covers fought to stay shut. *Crossing Jordan* and *Dragon Rider* clapped violently in resistance. But it was little use. The bits of souls eventually were wres-tled loose. They were all sucked down by the Blue Queen, who was now as full as a tick, blue and lit from within. She was so full, in fact, that she staggered for a moment.

Lucess jumped up and shut the trunk. "That's enough! You can't take any more."

The crowd grew quiet. The Blue Queen leaned on the back of Fattler's chair, and when she found her balance, she spoke with a voice like a loud, growling engine. "Of course I can! And later I will!"

Fern wondered if she would stop with just the books. Or would she use her powers to take the souls of all her followers? Fern remembered the terror of being under the bed in the Blue Queen's hotel room, her hands turning to books, the pull and drag on her own soul.

"Now!" the Blue Queen said. "Hand over the key, Fattler! Now that you really know who I am!"

Fattler stared out over the crowd. "I don't have it," he snapped, his face tight with anger.

The Blue Queen had enormous strength. She picked up Fattler, chair and all, and spun him around to face her. "Of course you do! Don't lie to me! I want that key now!"

"I don't know where it is!" Fattler said.

Lucess was sitting on the trunk. She'd retrieved her father's fishbowl and was cradling it in her lap, the three fish jostling. "I don't like this," she said. "Stop, please."

But her mother, torch-lit and reeling with her own enormous heft, ignored her. "The key, now. So that I can move on to your death."

"This is crazy! Listen," Fattler said, shaking his head nervously. "You'll never take over the Anybodies again. Even if you have the key to the castle, even if you're stronger than ever, even with this Secret Society to back you up. The Great Realdo will find a way to lead an uprising. The Anybodies will revolt. You'll be defeated again."

The Blue Queen started laughing. She laughed so hard and loud that it hurt Fern's ears. The crowd of Somebodies laughed along with her. Fattler glanced around nervously.

"Do you think that's all she's after?" a Somebody in the crowd shouted. "Ruling over the Anybodies?"

"You don't know anything about her powers!" another shouted.

Lucess spoke up too. "The plan's so much bigger than you think."

The Blue Queen shouted, "The soul of Willy Fattler is pretty powerless and weak these days. In fact, I'm surrounded by weak souls. You know, I don't have to rely only on books for souls, Fattler. That's the old me. I've invented a new way to get souls. A brand-spanking-new way! And I plan to unveil it *tonight*!"

The crowd roared. Fern knew that they shouldn't be so excited. She knew the Blue Queen's new way of gathering power. Fern clenched her fists so she wouldn't feel her hands stiffening into books, her fingers light as pages. She knew how powerful the Blue Queen had become.

"In fact there is one certain soul that I've been eyeing for years."

Fern felt heat creep up her neck and flush her face.

"Not . . . You don't mean. . . ," Fattler said.

"You know exactly the soul I'm talking about. You know. Don't you? Why don't you name her?"

"Not Fern," Fattler said. "Not her."

"Bingo!" the Blue Queen said. "Exactly! Let's go after the young, get rid of them before they become more of a nuisance."

Fern's heart started beating even harder, like hooves in her chest. She worried that the Somebodies would be able to hear it pounding away and would find her hiding in the hedgerow.

"Yes," the Blue Queen went on, "I'm sure that Fern is on her way! I'm looking forward to the power trapped in that young royal."

"It won't work," Fattler said. "Never!"

"Don't worry. It will work. My whole plan will work," she growled loudly, the motor revving as she pointed at the castle with her thick blue arms. "I will take the castle up! Straight *up*!"

The crowd of Somebodies let out a loud cheer.

Fern watched Fattler's eyes dart over the crowd. "Up? Why would you want to go up?"

"I'm going to rule over it all, Fattler. The city beneath the city *and* the city *above*! The castle itself is going to shoot straight up through the ground." She poked her finger in the air, her fingernail as sharp as the castle's steeple. "We will start by transforming New Yorkers into peasants. They'll be as weak as the Anybodies who were hypnotized by my speech today. Street by street, avenue by avenue, we will take them over. And I will rule! I will rule it all!"

Fern was stunned. She couldn't move. She imagined Central Park, the field that she'd thought of earlier with the family having its picnic. She imagined the castle shooting up through the sky of dirt, through the rocky geography, up, up, up, into Central Park itself. Could New Yorkers be turned into peasants? Could they be bossed and bullied and herded? Well, Fern only had to think for a moment about this, because, as you know if you've been to New York, New Yorkers are already herded, by one another, quite naturally, in and out of subways, across crosswalks, up and down elevators, in and out of fashion. How long before the most ambitious New Yorkers wanted to be big and quite blue? Hours, minutes, seconds?

"The key, Fattler!" the Blue Queen demanded. "I need the key!"

"For the last time, I DO NOT HAVE THE KEY!" Fattler shouted so loudly and with such vigorous anger that the crowd went silent, as if it dawned on them suddenly that maybe Fattler really didn't have the key. What then?

Overhead in the distance, Fern heard the screeching—the terrible, eerie, warbled screeches of the flying monkeys. She watched them circle overhead, and she could see what one of them had in its claws: a piggy bank with one fat leg.

The Blue Queen raised her eyes straight up. "What is this?" she said. "What have we here?"

THE BATTLE FORETOLD

EVERYONE'S EYES WERE NOW FIXED ON THE flying monkeys, their wings paddling through the damp night air: Fattler, roped to the chair; Lucess, holding on to her father's fishbowl; the Blue Queen, gasping with hope. Fern kept her eyes on the one with Howard-as-a-piggy-bank in its grip. It turned its wings and careened over the mound. What happened next seemed like it was in slow motion. She watched the flying monkey's talons open, and Howard-as-a-piggy-bank falling, falling, toward the mound.

Fern stood up in the hedgerow. Fattler saw her first. He'd been distracted by the flying monkeys even as the miniature pony was gnawing on the ropes behind his

back. Fern didn't think about what she should do. She just started running toward the mound.

Howard's shiny ceramic coat shone in the torchlight. His ceramic eyes looked terrified. He fell in the direction of the Blue Queen, but it was clear that she wouldn't be able to catch him with her big, blue, ungainly arms. Howard seemed to pick up speed as he fell. Fern dived, arms outstretched. She wasn't alone. The Brainkeeper and the two maids dived to catch Howard too.

They all landed hard on their ribs. Fern's chin struck the ground, and she closed her eyes tight for a second. She heard a terrible thud and crack. When she opened her eyes, she realized that her hands were empty. So were the Brainkeeper's and the two maids'.

Howard-as-a-piggy-bank lay between them on the grassy mound, now only shards of pottery. His hollow belly was broken into about ten thick pieces. His face was the only thing to remain whole—his snout pointed at Fern, his eyes a blank stare. Fern let out a small pop of air from her lungs, a sob. Her eyes flooded with tears. "He's gone," she whispered. Howard! She'd put him in danger. She'd sacrificed him—just like Dorathea had sacrificed her brother Merton—in the hope of somehow saving everyone. But it didn't seem worth it. Saving everyone didn't even seem possible now. And Howard was gone. Gone!

The Brainkeeper was crying too.

The exploded-bun maid said, "Maybe if we collect the pieces . . ."

The wrestler woman said, "Maybe we can glue them . . ."

Fern wasn't listening. A fat blue arm appeared overhead, reached into the broken glass and grabbed a long white ivory key! Fern hadn't spotted the key until that moment; it had been lost to her, white on white. She watched the key, now in the grip of a blue fist, shoot up over the Blue Queen's large round head.

"Yes!" the Blue Queen shouted. "Yes! It belongs to me! To me! And, look, Fern has shown up as well. Just in time!"

The Secret Society of Somebodies was screaming with joy now, shouting and whooping.

Fattler looked defeated and weak, but, if anyone had looked closely, they would have noticed one arched eyebrow, and the miniature pony breaking through the ropes.

The Blue Queen's arm came down again. Fern could see it swooping toward her.

"Run," Fattler said, seeing it too.

The Brainkeeper tried to shove the Blue Queen out of the way. The maids grabbed on to her skirts. But she was so powerful that she whipped them off into the crowd.

Fern didn't have time to run. She could only scramble downhill.

The Blue Queen stomped after her.

Fern, on her hands and knees, reached the bottom of the mound, where the Somebodies were still hooting and cheering.

The arm came down again, and that's the moment Fern felt something under her hand—it was round and small. She grabbed it, and as the Blue Queen swept her up and away, she could see what it was: one of Howard's sample minibottles of Correct-O-Cure. Since it had been in his pocket, it must have wound up alongside the ivory key in his hollow piggy-bank belly and then rolled downhill when he broke. Fern grabbed hold of it with all her might, and she thought back to what Howard had said when she'd called it a scam: *Everyone has to have faith in something.*

Fern shouted to Fattler while kicking and fighting the Blue Queen's hold as she was being hauled off to the castle. "Remember! You are a genius, Fattler!"

"Fern," Fattler shouted. "Fern! No, don't take her!" He wrestled the last of the ropes free and ran toward her.

The Brainkeeper and the maids tried to make it through the crowd too.

"Hold them back!" the Blue Queen shouted. "Hold them back!"

The crowd pushed in around Fattler and the Brainkeeper and the maids, grabbing their arms.

The Blue Queen passed by Lucess and grabbed the fishbowl from her. "I'll take this!"

"No!" Fern shouted, watching water lap over the edge of the bowl. The three fish—Merton, Dorathea, and the Bone—were sloshing around inside.

The Blue Queen turned to the crowd again. "Hold this one back too," she said, meaning her daughter. This confused the Somebodies, but two of them did as they were told and took Lucess's arms.

"Mother!" Lucess cried out. "You can't go without me! I'm coming!" She struggled. "I'm coming! Wait!"

The Blue Queen ignored her.

The crowd was so thick now—all of them collected around the Blue Queen as she ascended the marbled stairs to the entrance, with Fern in one arm, the goldfish bowl in the other, and her blue fist holding the key. Fern didn't fight too hard now. She knew this was inevitable. She had to battle the Blue Queen.

The Blue Queen stared out into the crowd with something that looked like love or kinship, but it wasn't. "Oh, look at all of you with your cow eyes, gazing at me! Gazing! Oh, my underlings! Let's unveil the new way of stealing souls right here, right now. With you. I'm ready for boost number one!"

She raised her hands in the air. She threw back her head.

Fern gasped. "No!" she shouted.

But the Somebodies in the front of the circle had already begun to change. Their hands were pulled from their sides. They flapped open like books, and their souls glowed there in the lit pages skittering in the wind. Their eyes grew wild with fear. The other Somebodies nearby pushed away and watched in horror as the souls quivered and then were released. The Blue Queen gulped them down greedily. And the bodies grew weak. They slumped to the ground.

Fern heard Fattler shout, and then saw him bucking

away from the Somebodies who'd been trying to hold him down. He shook loose and ran to a clear spot on the lawn, where he transformed the Somebodies whose souls were still being pulled from them, as well as a few standing close to them, into bronze statues—the kind one might find spitting water in a fancy hotel fountain. (Fattler's imagination was always hotel oriented.) He glared up at the flying monkeys who'd been circling above, and they fell to the ground with the weight of bronze. One lost a wing, the other a tail.

The Brainkeeper and the two maids looked at him, quite stunned.

"I am Willy Fattler, you know!" he said.

The Blue Queen didn't like the quick turn of events. Before Fattler could do any more, she fit the ivory key into the lock and twisted the black iron knob. The huge, heavy door swung slowly open.

"Mother!" Lucess cried, surrounded by Somebodies who were dazed by what had just happened. "Wait for me!" Lucess shouted.

The Blue Queen slammed the large door shut with a final *gong*.

4

THE CASTLE

PINNED UNDER THE BLUE QUEEN'S MONSTROUS arm, Fern held on tightly to Howard's sample mini-bottle spray of Correct-O-Cure. She knew it didn't work. She knew it! And yet she couldn't let it go. Howard would want her to have some hope that it might help. Howard! Were the maids right? Could he be fixed? Fern was heartbroken and angry—at herself mostly, but also at the Blue Queen.

From her awkward view in the clutches of the Blue Queen, Fern seemed to be looking at the castle upside down. The castle had been left empty for eleven years, and so Fern wasn't surprised that it was dark and cold and musty. She was surprised, however, that as the Blue Queen walked over the threshold and flung one arm into the air, the wall sconces lit up, the dust and cobwebs fizzled away to nothing, and the marble floor and the gold walls took on a freshly scrubbed shine. The Blue Queen was still powerful even though she'd missed out on the souls of the Somebodies on the lawn.

"So good to be home again!" she said, leaning heavily against the door. "I'm going to put you down," the Blue Queen said. "No need to run. The whole place is sealed up!"

As the Blue Queen flipped Fern over to stand her on her feet, the apple fell out of her pocket and rolled across the floor.

"What's this?" the Blue Queen asked, picking up the apple.

"My last meal?" Fern said with a shrug, hoping that the Blue Queen wouldn't register that it wasn't an apple at all, but was really something quite valuable: *The Art of Being Anybody* by Oglethorp Henceforthtowith.

The Blue Queen tossed the apple high into the air. Fern watched it rise up and fall. The Blue Queen caught it. She was on to Fern now. She knew that the apple meant something to her. "This apple," she said "sure looks sweet!"

"I guess so," Fern said.

The Blue Queen led Fern to a parlor where, with a quick wave, the dusty, yellowed sheets flipped off the plush wingback chairs and divans and love seats.

Embroidered curtains dropped from gold rods above the windows and draped themselves. The room instantly gleamed. Fern wondered if the Blue Queen was already strong enough to take the castle straight up. Could such a thing be done?

Fern had been thinking about the castle for a long time. Did it belong to her? She was royalty, wasn't she? She looked up into the oil paintings that hung on the wall: a pheasant hunt, a man in a captain's suit, a woman with a wrinkled nose. It didn't seem like home to her. Fern noticed the large windows. They were barred, and through the bars, the eager faces of Somebodies peered inside. She didn't belong here at all.

She tried another tack. "Nice place," Fern said calmly, even though she didn't feel calm at all. She didn't look at the apple.

"It is, isn't it." The Blue Queen looked at Fern. "Stop staring at me!" the Blue Queen said. "Stop gawking with those big, ugly eyes!" She fiddled with her larvae-moth brooch nervously with one hand, and then anxiously plucked the short stem out of the top of the apple.

Fern looked away, but liked how she'd made the Blue Queen uncomfortable. It gave Fern enough confidence to ask a question. "What are they doing out there?" She pointed at the Somebodies.

"Who cares!" the Blue Queen said, peeling a small

sticker off the apple. "I never intended to give them any real power. I only need them for a boost from a stolen soul now and then."

"What about Lucess?"

"What about her?" the Blue Queen said flatly.

"Are you just going to leave her?"

"Lucess is too squeamish. Too weak. Like her father," she said, tapping the fishbowl. "A loveless man, in the end. He turned me in to that awful sister of his!" She leaned in to look at the three fish spinning in the bowl. She said, "And now you're paying for it, aren't you!" She smiled at the fish devilishly and touched the brooch. The brooch. Fern hadn't paid much attention to it until now. What was that brooch? Why did she touch it just then, in such a knowing way?

The Blue Queen turned back to Fern. "Lucess would be more of a problem than she's worth. You've seen her with her sniveling love, with her *Wait for me.* She would only disappoint me, like her father." She glanced at Fern again, and began rubbing the apple on her shirt.

Remembering what the Blue Queen had said to Lucess, *Don't have friends,* Fern repeated the rest to herself out loud: "Have underlings! Friends only disappoint."

"Correct!" the Blue Queen said, rubbing the apple more vigorously.

"And that goes double for husbands and daughters."

"Yes, of course!" She glared at Fern. "Is this a poison apple, Fern? Have you come here to try to kill me? Now, that would be disappointing!"

"Maybe it is," Fern said. "I don't know for sure."

"Why don't you eat it, Fern? Here. Go ahead." She shoved the apple at Fern.

The Somebodies, alarmed and distraught that their leader had turned on them, had started banging on the windows. The Blue Queen ignored them. "Take a bite!"

"I once knew someone," Fern said, stalling, hoping that among the faces popping up at the windows, she would see Fattler or the Brainkeeper, "who made Abstract Origami."

The Blue Queen said, "Take a bite!"

"And," Fern said, not sure where she was going with all of this, "and . . ." She ran to a large oak desk with a blotter and blank paper next to an inkwell. She grabbed a piece of paper. "And he made art from the paper by doing this." She turned the paper, twisted it, bent it, tore it a bit and then presented it to the Blue Queen.

"Crumpled paper. So what? Stop wasting my time!"

"No, it isn't bent-up paper. It's a family," Fern said. "It's a mother and a father and a daughter in an open field, having a picnic. They're happy. They love one another, even though they won't really be a family like that forever."

The Blue Queen stopped and stared at the Abstract Origami. It seemed to have caught her attention. She was stalled.

"You weren't faking being happy at your wedding, were you?" Fern asked. "You were actually happy."

"Stop looking at me with those big, ugly eyes. I told you to stop!"

Fern didn't stop. "You were actually in love with Merton Gretel."

"Shut those awful eyes!" the Blue Queen shouted. "Take a bite!"

Fern pressed on. "And you love Lucess, too, don't you? You just don't want to risk showing it."

"Bite the apple, Fern!"

And so Fern did bite the apple, a small bite. It tasted like dust and ink and binding glue. She chewed a bit. "Not bad," Fern said, looking at the Blue Queen wide-eyed.

"I will fix those eyes," the Blue Queen said, ripping the Abstract Origami of the family at the picnic. She walked to the curtains, bit into the cloth, then ripped a long narrow swatch with her teeth.

The Blue Queen grabbed Fern again by the arm and wrapped the cloth around Fern's eyes. The room went dark, everything slipped from view—the plush divans, the oil paintings, the eager faces of Somebodies staring sharply through the windows. And suddenly the Blue Queen was only a voice and a cold, hard hold on Fern's arm. She pushed Fern into an armchair, and Fern could feel the room grow windy. The light slipping in at the edge of her blindfold went dim. Fern knew that the Blue Queen was raising her arms, preparing to swallow Fern's soul—and not just a small piece of it. She was planning to swallow it whole. Fern at last swallowed the bite of apple with a panicked gulp.

Fern held tight to the arms of the chair and pushed herself back into it. "No," she said. "You can't!" But suddenly Fern wasn't as scared as she had been. She knew, deeply, from the center of her being, that she would defeat the Blue Queen. The notion spread from her middle up to her brain, and she could see the words, read them: "Fern Defeats the Blue Queen." Had she eaten that part of *The Art of Being Anybody*? Had she ingested history?

Fern knew she had only one way to defend herself. As if it had been written out somewhere, she knew to pick up Howard's sample minibottle of Correct-O-Cure. She sprayed it in the direction of the Blue Queen's whisper.

The Blue Queen only laughed. "Is that what royalty has to resort to these days? Is that the best you've got?"

Fern pulled the spray bottle back to her chest. Her

other hand was losing its grip on the arm of the chair. In fact, that hand was suddenly stiff and could no longer hold on. Fern lifted her hand up, and she could feel the two hard edges, and hear the light shuffling of pages.

Her hand was no longer a hand. It was a book, just as it had been under the bed in Willy Fattler's Underground Hotel. Fern could feel her book-hand pushing open. She tried to shut it, to pull it in to her chest, but the Blue Queen's pull was too strong. A small bit of her soul tore free of the book.

And that's the moment when the castle started to rumble and shake.

The pictures fell off the walls, their glass shattered. Furniture jiggled against the floor. Windows broke. Some of the flooring in one corner tore away from the ground, leaving a jagged hole.

Fern felt another bit of soul rip away, and this time the castle grumbled and muscled upward, grinding through dirt and rock. She lost another bit of her soul and then another and each time, the castle inched its way up and up.

Fern panicked. She could feel herself growing weak. *No*, she thought, *it can't be. My soul is mine. There is something about me that never changes. There's something about me that I can always count on.* She thought of Howard, broken to pieces on the dirt mound. Why had she jumped out of her hiding place to save him? Why had she shown up at the Secret Society of Somebodies at all?

The answers came to her: she wanted to save Howard; she wanted to save the Anybodies. They were real people.

She yelled out to the Blue Queen, "You'll *never* be royal! Not really! Not ever! Because you rule over underlings, not people."

The Blue Queen was growing stronger every second. Her rage seemed to fuel the castle, pushing its way up like a sharp tooth.

"We've broken ground!" the Blue Queen shouted joyfully.

And she was right. In the middle of Central Park, in an open field, the castle's black spire needled through to the other side and was now poking up. It kept forcing its way upward, trembling the ground around it, until the very windows of the tower at the top of the castle were showing.

There was only one person in this part of Central Park, at this moment in the middle of the night: an anxious young man, who'd been feeling weak and feverish ever since a mysterious incident in a donut shop. And now for the extremely coincidental part of this story—

this anxious young man was, in fact, N. E. Bode, which is to say, me. I was cutting across Central Park to get to my favorite all-night pharmacy, where I was going to explain my maladies to the pharmacist, who doesn't speak much English, but who is, nonetheless, a good listener. I was in disguise as a Canadian and was already feeling highly foreign myself. In fact, with all my disguises—the endless parade of N. E. Bode—I was starting to forget who I really was.

And so I was already asking deep questions when I happened upon this odd sight. *Is this art?* I wondered. The new kind that is meant to make people uncomfortable? *Is this reality television?* I wondered. (My newfound Canadian tastes made me resent America's zeal for reality television.) Am I going to be embarrassed on national television? Have I wandered onto a movie set? Is Glenn Close about to pop out of a trailer and ask for a cup of coffee?

No. The answer to all of this is: No. I was sick, I reminded myself; I was fevered and hallucinating. I'd have to tell the pharmacist this. Maybe I'd draw a picture. But as I padded on across the park, I thought, *There is something very wrong here. Something terrible. Something truly awful,* and I felt a terrible coldness seep up through the soles of my shoes, up my legs, and the coldness burrow into my heart.

Meanwhile Fern, with all the fragile breath in her lungs, pushed out one final phrase, "No, you'll only be a ruler—never royal."

She wasn't sure of what happened to her after this. The sample minibottle of Correct-O-Cure grew thicker and heavier in her hand. It was long, like a pole, with more weight on one end. Fern could almost place the object, but not quite. She'd held this before, but what was it?

Fern could suddenly see dimly through the blindfold. In fact, the blindfold grew hard, stiff, and too loose to fit around her eyes. Weighty, too, it slipped off her face and landed on her chest. It was big and gold, and it sat like a giant ring around her neck. She glanced up and saw that the sample minibottle had turned into her scepter. The loose gold ring around her neck was, in fact, her oversized crown. Fern wasn't sure what to do, but she felt stronger.

She could now see the Blue Queen, who was so big that her head was touching a chandelier. Fern held her scepter over her head, and she wished that the Correct-O-Cure weren't a sham, that it was real. She thought, *You can't count on that stuff working. You can only count on yourself in times like these.* And that's when Fern's scepter let out a hissing steam that smelled like burnt plastic. It shot up over Fern's head and clouded

the Blue Queen's face. She coughed and gagged. The castle came to a trembling stop.

Then the Blue Queen began shrinking. She grew smaller and paler until she was the size of a normal woman. She tumbled backward and caught herself for a moment on the edge of a chair before falling to the floor. Her skin was so pale that it seemed to shine. Fern lifted the crown off her chest and set it on the back of her head. She walked over to the Blue Queen.

"Hello?" Fern said. "Hello?"

The Blue Queen's eyes were closed, her mouth open; and the first white moth crawled up from her lips slowly. It perched there for a moment and then flittered up and around the room. It surprised Fern, this white moth. She watched it flit around, and it made Fern think of the egg-shaped pills, the souls in the jars, and how they'd become caterpillars and then must have woven cocoons. Was this moth a bit of a soul?

More moths followed, lifting up from her mouth and batting through the cloud of Correct-O-Cure spray.

When Fern looked back at the Blue Queen, shrunken and pale, all the cocoons on the brooch pinned to her chest had broken open, setting loose even more moths. The one in the middle flitted its wings, and all of them, one by one, skittered to the fishbowl, where they perched on the bowl's lip. The goldfish who was

Merton Gretel swam to the surface. He stared up at the ring of moths—all the lost bits of his soul—and he raised his fish mouth to the surface of the water. He opened his mouth as wide as he could. The moths rose up and sifted down into his mouth, and with each one, Fern said, "Merton Gretel!"

His face appeared first—a man's face on a fish's gold body. And then his front fins turned into hands. With them he reached up to the top edges of the bowl and pulled himself out. He grew and grew. His back fins flipped into feet. His scales turned into a goldish suit. The black spot under his fish eye turned into a mole. His glasses were the last thing to appear. He pushed them up on his bent nose, and Fern came into focus.

"Hello there," he said. "Merton Gretel's the name."

Fern was too stunned to answer. She mustered a happy nod. She stared at the two remaining fish. Would they be saved too? Fern and Merton turned their attention to the Blue Queen. Moth after moth was rising up from her mouth. A burst of them made their dizzy path to the edge of the fishbowl, where Dorathea and the Bone took back their souls. And, like Merton, they sprouted arms, lifted themselves from the bowl and turned back into themselves. Fern was relieved. She sighed with joy and weariness. Dorathea and the Bone's mouths stopped pursing. They rubbed their dry arms.

They were surprised to see themselves as themselves again.

Then they spotted Fern and nearly rushed to hug her, but they were stopped by the sight of a number of moths perched on Fern's shoulders. These moths seemed to be familiar to Fern. Pieces of her soul? Could it be? Fern cupped one in her hand. She felt its wings brushing her fingers. When she raised her hand to look at the moth inside, the moth was gone, and Fern felt stronger. It was hard to explain. She did the same thing with the next moth perched on her shoulder, and the next . . . until they were all gone, until she felt all better.

The Blue Queen was still shrinking. Her eyes opened for a moment and she said one word:

"Picnic."

And then, as if this were a final release, a stream of moths poured from her mouth—more and more, until moths filled the air like a snowstorm.

THE HOLE LEFT BEHIND

AND WHAT HAPPENED TO FATTLER, THE BRAIN-
keeper, the two maids, the miniature pony, Lucess
Brine, the Somebodies, and the flying monkeys? What
happened to Howard, broken into all those pieces still
sitting on the grassy mound of the castle's lawn?

Well, Fattler's anger with the Somebodies grew. He
hated their clamoring for the Queen who had betrayed
them, tired of their bullying grips on his arms, tired of
their snotty comments. He didn't like the way they
treated the Brainkeeper, who was a nice guy, after all—
a better beekeeper than Brainkeeper, but sometimes
people get miscast in life. And he didn't like the way
they treated the maids, as if the maids were servants,

which, Fattler supposed, they were. But that was no reason to treat them badly. He didn't like the way they treated Lucess. She was just a child—a child whose mother was no good and who'd just abandoned her. Lucess was still crying. And one of the Somebodies was holding the pony roughly by his mane.

And so, after Fern was hauled inside by the Blue Queen and battling away, Fattler took care of the rest of the Somebodies, turning them all into a field of bronze statues.

The exploded-bun woman was the one to point out the problem. "Well, sir, you've frozen them while they've got hold of us. I mean I can't get out of a bronze grip."

"Sorry!" Fattler said quickly. He turned the bronze statues into rubber ones, and the maids slipped free.

Lucess stared up at the castle, tears streaming down her face. "My father!" she said. "My daddy!"

By this point the castle had ripped itself up from the dirt and was on the rise. The two maids, Fattler, and the Brainkeeper didn't waste much time looking at the castle—Fern would have to handle that. They rushed to Howard-as-a-piggy-bank, knelt down and began trying to see if the pieces would fit back together.

"Can you fix this?" the Brainkeeper asked Fattler.

Fattler shook his head. "I'm not so sure that I can."

The castle was shoving its way up, dropping parts of

itself on the way. It lost chunks of retaining walls. Wires dangled from it and quivered behind. It left a hole. A big one.

They all looked up at the castle. The bottom floor glowed bluish. They could see the Blue Queen growing bigger and broader through the barred windows.

"Do you think Fern can do it?" Fattler asked.

"I have faith in her," said the Brainkeeper.

The maids nodded in unison. "Me too."

The pony was shaking. The exploded-bun maid picked it up and cradled it like a baby.

And just at that moment, the blue room filled with a kind of steam, and the blueness of the room faded. The castle nudged another inch and then stopped. The steam formed a cloud that floated out the windows and over the lawn, and settled on the grassy mound, on the pieces of Howard scattered there. It was the spray from the Correct-O-Cure bottle that had turned into Fern's scepter, and it stunk of burnt plastic.

Howard's pieces began to seal together, and then the whole pig began to grow and soften and become fleshy. His snout shrunk to his normal nose. His hair sprouted on his head. The slit on his back disappeared. His clothes wove over him.

And that was when the moths started to pour from the windows of the first floor of the castle. A fine dusting of moths lighting down. They flitted to the pile of dead books left on the mound. They burrowed into their pages, one after the other. And there was another batch of moths that headed across the wide lawn and flitted above the fishpond, where the fish rose to the surface—ten of them, in fact. They swallowed the moths and grew back into people.

Fattler was the one who started recognizing them. "That's Olaf Chang! And the Borscht Duo, Todd and Irv!"

"And Ernst Flank," the exploded-bun maid said. "And Marilynn Partridge, Carlita Cole, Marge 'the Boss' Carter."

The wrestler maid continued. "Jive McMurtry, Erma Harris, Albert Jones-Jones! They're all alive!"

It was the rest of those on the list of the dead from the Eleven-Day Reign. But they weren't dead after all.

"Maybe she didn't have the heart to kill them," the Brainkeeper said.

"They're back!" Lucess said, her voice brimming with hope.

Fattler, the Brainkeeper, the maids, and Lucess all stood there in silence, waiting for what might happen next. They turned their attention back to the castle, where two legs appeared—Fern's two legs. She jumped from the first floor doorway and landed on the ground.

"Lucess," she called. "Lucess!"

Lucess looked up. "What?" she asked.

"Your father!" Fern shouted. "He's here!" A man jumped down from the doorway. It was Lucess's father. Used to swimming, he walked unsteadily. Lucess pulled free of the frozen Somebodies and ran to him.

"Daddy!" she cried. "You're back!"

"Lulu," her father said. "My Lulu!"

Then Fern saw Howard, standing there with his arms folded on his chest proudly. He stepped toward Fern, favoring his bee-stung leg. And he said, "Well, well, well. Correct-O-Cure."

Fern grabbed him and hugged. "I had to have faith in something," she said.

EPILOGUE

DEAR READER,

Not all of the mothy souls flittered back to their respective books. No, no. Some of them dithered upward to the top of the castle, straight up to the room situated beneath the spire. It was a small, circular room, its windows now broken. The spire had pierced through the rock and dirt, bullying its way so that the high windows in the small circular room were above ground, with a view of a field and some large rocks and trees and a distant bike path. The mothy souls escaped through these windows and floated off on gusty breezes.

They had homing abilities too, but instead of finding their authors by way of books, they took the bolder approach of just trying to find the authors themselves. I was still disguised as a Canadian, and was walking home from my all-night pharmacy with a bottle of aspirin. My pharmacist always suggested aspirin. I'd already uncapped the bottle and pulled out the fluffy cotton. I was standing there, thinking, *Who is N. E. Bode? Is his life no more real than this fluff of cotton? Has his fear of being found out by his insanely jealous creative writing professor come to rule his life?* And then I let the cotton go and watched it land in the gutter, where it slipped down a grate. Some Canadians were approaching and, afraid that they'd want to talk to me about Canadian things, I turned in the opposite direction.

I turned quickly, and that's when I saw the moth for a brief second. It had been following closely, and so there it was right in front of my face. Right in front of my mouth, in fact. I gasped. By which I mean, I swallowed it. Straight down the gullet. It tickled a bit, sure. But as soon as it was down, I felt better. I felt like I'd been missing something without knowing it and now it was back! And, of course, that was exactly what had happened.

My soul was mended—whole again.

But! This probably doesn't answer all your questions. Let's take it from the top.

Did Dorathea and the Bone and Fern and Howard

ever get to grab each other and hug each other as tightly as they could and say all the things they needed to say?

Yes, yes. Once Fern had hugged Howard there on the front lawn, they turned and looked at Dorathea and the Bone, who'd made it out of the castle as well. And they did heartily grab each other and hug each other, and they started crying, all of them, quite messily.

"You saved us!" the Bone said to Fern.

"You're brave, Fern," Dorathea said. "You saved the Anybodies because of your good, strong soul—so pure and true! That's the most royal part of you!"

Fern and Howard were, at this point, swallowed up in Dorathea's and the Bone's arms. Fern's face was right next to Howard's face. She smiled at him, and he smiled back. It was one of those moments when you couldn't hold in a smile if you tried your mightiest to do so.

The Bone said to Howard, "You were brave, too!"

Dorathea added, "We're so proud of you both!"

Was Dorathea happy to have found that her brother wasn't dead, that he'd been brought back from the form of a goldfish? She was. Again, there was relief, joy and messy crying. She walked up to her brother, closed her eyes, cupped her hand to his ear and whispered something.

He smiled, pushed his glasses up his nose and said, "Me too." Had they said they missed each other, that they loved each other? Probably yes to both.

The Blue Queen? Yes, yes. You'll want to know about the Blue Queen. Not dead. She was once again stripped of all of her powers and is now recuperating in an Anybody hospital where she is undergoing treatment by a therapist who specializes in issues about lost love and egomania and soul-swallowing.

And Fattler. It turns out that he is a genius, but he's ordinary, too. An ordinary genius. And like all people, he did need help. He made a team—the exploded-bun maid, the wrestler woman, the Brainkeeper—who set up with his own beekeeping apparatus to manufacture Willy Fattler's Sweet Honey, available in jars for $6.99 in the gift shop.

What about the Somebodies he turned into rubber

statues? The transformations wore off slowly. They turned back into themselves, one at a time. They each looked around, noting the castle with its bottom hanging in the dirt sky, and they decided to brush off their pants, take off their SSS robes, and return to their lives. A little disenchanted, but a little relieved, too.

Now, one of you wants to know whether the miniature pony made it back to Mrs. Fluggery's hairdo. No. The miniature humpbacked pony became Fern and Howard's pet.

And speaking of those two, did they have to go to Gravers Military Academy?

Well, did they?

Gravers Military Academy does have some standards. They draw the line at runaways. *Sorry,* the officials said, *we just won't take them.* Too much of a liability.

As for all those other people we met along the way?

Fern thinks of them often. As it turns out, she learned an awful lot from them. If I were the kind of writer to try to teach my readers lessons, I'd say something like: suffer fools gladly, because a bad example can be as valuable as a good one. I'd say something about the importance of sticking with your dreams.

The elevator operator with his shiny buttons, he's stopped letting his fears rule him and he's in engineering school. Here is a photo of him with his slide rule! He's already designed some new glass elevator lines.

And Hyun-Arnold has had success as well. He's set up a counseling service called Sage Advice in the back of Hyun's Dollar Fiesta. He can't hang up the Korean accent—it makes him think more clearly, as it turns out—or the pricing (all advice is one dollar), but he feels like he's being truer to his talents.

Now, there's one more nagging issue, isn't there?

You want to know the answer to this question: If you go deep into Central Park to a certain spot, will you find a spire pointing out of the ground and, beneath it, a tower room with broken windows?

Fattler and Dorathea teamed up to fix this. They went to Central Park the night of the battle with the Blue Queen. They were cloaked in darkness, as they say in those kinds of books where people go about cloaked in darkness. They considered turning the spire into a giant tree with a massive base, but they didn't want to tamper with the castle. It seemed historic really, this moment of the city beneath the city crossing into the city above the city. And so instead they used their Anybody's powers to cover the spire and the tower room with the giant hull of a massive tree. If you go to Central Park and find this certain tree, you will recognize it by a ring of knotholes. Inside the knotholes there is the ring of windows around the tower, so that light can still stream inside it.

In the city beneath the city, on the grounds below, where the uprooted castle dangled, they worded a plaque—THE BATTLE OF FERN AND THE BLUE QUEEN—and they etched in the date. The plaque showed up in Fern's book *The Art of Being Anybody*, which, once transformed back into itself, still smelled like apple for quite some time and had a few permanent teeth marks on the binding. It had to regrow the section on Fern's battle with the Blue Queen, but it did eventually come back—a full account in Henceforthtowith's confusing prose.

And what about me? What about N. E. Bode? How is he now? Isn't someone asking that question?

Well, no more disguises necessary. Oddly enough, I've found the perfect hideout. It has a view of Central Park—some trees, some rocks, a distant bike path. The light streams in through the windows. I think you know the spot I mean. I go to Jubber's Pork Rind Juke Joint on Wednesdays for their All-U-Can-Eat Pork Rind special. I get my shirts starched at Melvin's Laundromat and Dry Cleaner's, and I recently won seventeen dollars playing bingo at Blessed Holy Trinity Church and Bingo Hall. When I'm feeling fancy, I order a duck in blue cream sauce, now available at Willy Fattler's Undergound Hotel dining room. And I buy my items—invisible flower pots, tins of smelts, musical filing cabinets—at Hyun's Dollar Fiesta, where I also purchase sage advice, often in bulk.

If you happen by such a giant tree in Central Park, noting the ring of knotholes, you might want to knock on the bark. If I'm in, I will knock back. In fact, let's have a secret knocking code. You knock twice fast then three times slow then fifteen times in stutter order, hard, soft, hard, soft. And I'll knock back the same way. This way you can be sure that you're communicating with me—and not some other person living beneath a spire in a tower room hidden in a giant tree with knotholes, halfway in the city beneath the city and halfway in the city above.

On second thought, a normal knock might do.

Sincerely (and I mean that!),

NE Bode